"John Adamos isn't [...] is it?"

"Why do you ask?"

"It doesn't feel like my name. There's no recognition, no connection."

"No. It's not your real name." Her eyes flicked down to her own cup, then back up to his. A veil had dropped over her eyes. The woman in front of him was even more of a stranger than the one he had happened upon down on the beach. Cool, collected.

Withdrawn.

"Your name is Julius Carvalho."

Something flickered inside him, a flame of recognition. Distant, but there.

"Julius," he repeated.

"Yes." She breathed in deeply. "Crown Prince Julius Adamos Carvalho."

Silence stretched between them once more. Laughter died in his throat as he saw the seriousness in her eyes.

"Prince," he echoed.

"Yes. Heir to the throne of the island nation of Rodina."

Diamonds of the Rich and Famous

London's most exclusive jeweler.
Three life-changing gems.

If you're part of the glitterati, then you've already heard of Smyth's, London's most exclusive—and elusive—purveyor of diamonds. But recently new rumors have been swirling around the brilliant boutique: these flawless gems seem to generate drama!

PA Mareka is just picking up a ring for her CEO boss when a run-in with the paparazzi has the world convinced she's his bride! The papers think they're a perfect match: could they be right?

Find out in Mareka and Caye's story

Accidentally Wearing the Argentinian's Ring
by Maya Blake

After an accident, Julius wakes with an engagement ring fit for royalty as the only clue to his identity— the Crown Prince of Rodina! But who is his betrothed?

Read more in Esme and Julius's story

Prince's Forgotten Diamond by Emmy Grayson

Both available now!

After one scorching night together, billionaire Saint Montgomery wants to give mysterious Fliss a jewel to remember him by. But he's already left her with quite the memento—she's pregnant!

Don't miss Fliss and Saint's story

Coming soon from Dani Collins!

Prince's Forgotten Diamond

EMMY GRAYSON

HARLEQUIN

PRESENTS

HARLEQUIN® PRESENTS™

Recycling programs for this product may not exist in your area.

ISBN-13: 978-1-335-59353-5

Prince's Forgotten Diamond

Harlequin Enterprises ULC
22 Adelaide St. West, 41st Floor
Toronto, Ontario M5H 4E3, Canada
www.Harlequin.com

Printed in Lithuania

MIX
Paper | Supporting responsible forestry
FSC® C021394

Emmy Grayson wrote her first book at the age of seven about a spooky ghost. Her passion for romance novels began a few years later with the discovery of a worn copy of Kathleen Woodiwiss's *A Rose in Winter* buried on her mother's bookshelf. She lives in the Midwest countryside with her husband (who's also her ex-husband), their children and enough animals to start their own zoo.

Books by Emmy Grayson

Visit the Author Profile page
at Harlequin.com.

To my readers,
you're all simply wonderful.

CHAPTER ONE

HE CAME TO with a gasp, the act of inhaling sending a hundred sharp knives stabbing into his chest. He uttered an oath and froze. Gradually the pain subsided. Each breath still burned like the devil, but at least he could sit up.

The room spun. He gritted his teeth and closed his eyes, waited, then slowly opened them again. The world slowed enough that he was able to evaluate his surroundings, from the plush rug laid atop gleaming mahogany floors to the glittering chandelier hanging above his head. Cautiously, he turned his head. He was sitting on a tufted leather couch. A marble fireplace dominated the wall to his left, the space above the mantel decorated with a painting of Westminster Abbey's Gothic towers. To the right lay a massive bed on a raised dais, the mattress draped in a luxurious midnight comforter and a mound of artfully arranged pillows.

A distant honk made him wince. Whatever he'd been through had left him not only with an aching chest but a monstrous headache. He slid his fingers through his hair, pausing when he located a lump at the base of his skull.

What the hell happened?

He stood and made his way to the bathroom. He turned

on the faucet, cupped his hands to catch the blessedly cool water and splashed it over his skin.

He raised his head, his eyes flickering to the mirror, then back again as confusion tugged at him. Confusion that quickly morphed into shock.

The face staring back at him was that of a stranger.

His hand came up, his fingertips tracing a long cut that ran from the slight hollow beneath his cheek down into the light beard following the lines of his jaw. The man in the glass mirrored his actions. Brown eyes stared back at him, fatigued and ringed by shadows.

Unfamiliar.

Who am I?

The question skittered through his mind, but encountered only silence. Silence and a gaping void that seemed to stretch on with no end in sight. No memories existed beyond this moment.

Dread pulled at him, fingers tugging, grasping at his consciousness. With a resolve that came to him as naturally as breathing, he stopped it. Panic had no place here.

He filled his lungs with a deep, cleansing breath before walking back into the bedroom. A quick search yielded no wallet or cell phone. The only luggage was a canvas duffel bag with leather straps. The clothes inside were simple yet well made, the tags featuring luxury labels he somehow recognized even though he couldn't even recall his own name. A thick white envelope, concealed in an interior side pocket, yielded nearly ten thousand euros. Whoever he was, it appeared he had money.

Or had taken it from someone who did.

Uncomfortable with the thought, his hand went back up to that cut, his fingers pressing against the wound. The sharp prick of pain centered him, pulled him back from the edge of diving too far into speculation that would get him nowhere.

A glance out the window revealed elegant buildings of brick and white stone stacked side by side. Some were storefronts, while others appeared to be office buildings. But they all carried the unmistakable mark of wealth. Taxis, red double-decker buses and pedestrians hurried to and fro beneath a darkening sky.

London.

He was in London. Something else flitted through his mind, but it darted away before he could grasp it.

One step at a time, he told himself. *See if anyone else is here.*

He moved away from the window to the double doors of the room. He listened for a full minute before carefully opening the door to a large, airy hallway with several expensive-looking paintings hung on the ivory walls between doors marked with room numbers.

A hotel then. Had he been attacked in the room? No, that didn't make sense. Surely if he had been attacked in here his assailant would have grabbed the duffel or at least searched it.

The headache returned with a vengeance. Twenty minutes later, after taking some pain medication he'd found in the bathroom and resting on the couch, he felt well enough to conduct another search of the room. He surveyed the lavish furnishings with a sharpened gaze. A flash of black caught his eye. On the floor underneath the couch lay an onyx business card. As he knelt, something shifted in his chest. He knew the card, knew the elegant cursive would have a delicate silver filigree style. Threads of apprehension and excitement drifted through him as his fingers closed around it.

The card was heavy, the edges rounded. On one side the card simply read *Smythe's*. On the other was a street address with a series of numbers in the bottom left corner. Someone had written *Saturday, 7:30* in silver ink in the right corner.

A sense of urgency suddenly took him. This card, and the appointment, were important. He glanced at his wrist, only to find the skin pale where a watch should have been. He picked up the phone by the bed.

"Good evening, thank you for calling The Bancroft, Anthony speaking."

He mentally noted the name of the hotel.

"Hello, Anthony. Could you please provide me with the date and time?"

"Certainly, sir. Today is April the fifth, and the time is almost seven in the evening."

"Is today Saturday?"

"Yes, sir."

He decided to take one last leap.

"Thank you, Anthony. My last question: what's the name listed for my room?"

A pause followed. "Sir?"

"Just clarifying what name the reservation was made under."

"Of course, sir. The name we have on file is John Adamos."

A Greek surname. One that didn't feel or sound familiar.

"Thank you."

He hung up the phone.

John Adamos.

He said the name out loud, repeated it several times. Each time it sounded as alien as when he'd first heard it.

His eyes moved back to the card. He had thirty minutes before the appointment time listed on the card. He could call the police or take himself to a hospital. But the hospital could take hours of examinations and scans. While he would need to see a doctor eventually, the medicine made his pain manageable for now. The police would interview him, possibly take a photo and circulate it to the media as they investigated what had happened to him. Something else that would take time.

He tapped the card against his other hand. This route, however, could give him answers within the hour.

He picked up the phone and dialed again.

"Good evening and thank you for—"

"Anthony, it's… John again." The name tasted foreign on his tongue.

"Yes, sir."

"Would you please have a taxi ready for me in ten minutes?"

Fifteen minutes later, John stood on the sidewalk that ran alongside a terrace of elegant town houses. The one listed on the card resembled the others in the row with its white brick, arched windows and elegant pillars guarding the main entrance. But unlike the glossy mahogany doors that graced the other homes, this one's door differed with its midnight black coloring. There was no sign, though, no indication that the house was anything but a residence. He ascended the stairs and pressed the doorbell. Scarcely two seconds passed before the door opened to reveal a man. A very, very tall man who looked as if he'd been stuffed into the black suit he wore and didn't look very happy about it.

"Good evening."

The man said nothing.

"I have an appointment."

One bushy eyebrow raised up toward the man's broad forehead. John pulled the card out of his pocket.

"I—"

The man's face underwent a startling transformation as John held the card up. A smile creased his face as his mountainous shoulders relaxed.

"My apologies, sir. Admittance is only allowed when the card is produced." He stood back and gestured for John to come in. "Welcome to Smythe's."

John hesitated a moment. A flicker of something teased his mind: an image of a chandelier dripping in diamonds. A smoky, feminine voice.

Then it was gone.

He walked inside, careful to keep his face blank even as surprise filtered through him. The entry hall itself was stunning, with a wrought-iron railing curled intimately around a staircase that circled up, gleaming marble floors and paintings displayed on the wall. Not just any paintings, he realized, as information filled his mind. Renoir, Monet, Kahlo and Rembrandt, to name a few. If these were genuine, they would fetch millions at auction.

Yet of all the incredible things in the entry hall, it wasn't the art that froze him in place. It was the gleaming chandelier above his head.

Satisfaction shot through him and eased some of his tension. He had been here before.

"The elevator will take you up."

John turned to see the man, apparently a guard of some sort, gesturing toward a glass column in the center of the staircase. The guard pushed a button on the wall and a door in the column opened to reveal an elevator, the car made of the same black iron as the railing.

"Enjoy your visit."

The elevator ride was short and smooth. The door opened without a sound. John paused, his eyes sweeping and assessing everything that lay before him.

A short set of stairs led down to the tiled floor, the staircase flanked by marble pillars the same pale aqua as the walls. Mirrors trimmed in gold lined the room, making it feel twice as big. Glass cases stood every few feet along the perimeter of the room.

Jewelry cases, John realized as he descended the stairs. Every case contained artfully arranged jewelry, from loose stones to elegantly set necklaces, bracelets, earrings and rings sparkling with rubies, emeralds, sapphires and diamonds, even a crown.

"Hello, again."

The smoky voice from his memory slid over him, a voice designed to tempt and seduce. Yet, he noted as he turned, despite the inherent sexiness in the tones, he experienced nothing more than a casual flicker of interest.

A woman stood at the top of the stairs. A sleeveless black dress clung to her curves. Sleek ebony hair had been cut into a bob, the sharply cut fringe of bangs accentuating her striking cheekbones and large eyes.

"Welcome back, Mr. Adamos."

"Thank you."

She cocked her head to the side. A flirtatious smile flitted about her lips, but her eyes were shrewd.

"Is everything all right?"

He paused. Part of him wanted to dive straight into questioning. But a sixth sense urged him to proceed with caution, to test the waters and work up to his questions.

"Yes." He held up the card. "Saturday at seven thirty, yes?"

She stared at him for a long moment before descending

the stairs. Each step was sensual, hips swaying, fingers lingering on the banister. Yet when she met his gaze, he saw a strong, calculating woman behind the theater. Whoever Miss Smythe was, she was certainly no fool.

"Champagne?"

"No, thank you."

She gestured toward a mahogany desk set against one wall, a floor-to-ceiling mirror behind it and a set of tufted leather chairs in front. He waited until she circled the desk and sat before he took his seat. She pulled a drawer out and, judging by the soft ticks, typed in a code. A click sounded, followed by the whooshing of a door swinging open. She reached down below, then set a black box on the desk between them.

"As promised."

John stared at the box. Then, slowly, he opened the lid.

The diamond glittered up at him from a bed of black silk. It was a diamond unlike any he'd ever seen. Black dots peppered the inside of the jewel, some pinpoints of color, others swirling out in tiny patterns that reminded him of a night sky. Tiny drops of pearls and aquamarine stones circled it, the entire arrangement set atop a silver band polished to a perfect shine.

Classic. Elegant. Romantic.

Flame. Red, silky flame spilling across his fingers. A laugh that made his body hard even as it made his chest light to hear it, to know he had made her smile. And then a name, whispered with such affection his chest tightened. "Julius..."

"It's stunning."

A genuine smile flashed on Miss Smythe's ruby-red lips, fleeting but proud.

"Thank you. I don't have many clients who request a salt-and-pepper diamond. It was a challenge I thoroughly enjoyed."

"Salt-and-pepper diamond?"

One perfectly sculpted eyebrow arched up.

"Yes. As we discussed at your last appointment."

"Remind me again."

She pulled the ring from the bed of silk and held it up. "Also known as galaxy or celestial diamonds, salt-and-pepper diamonds used to be seen as undesirable. Flawed. The black spots you see are bits of carbon or minerals that didn't crystallize during the formation of the diamond. But as the world evolves, they're starting to be appreciated for their uniqueness." She angled the ring so he could stare into the depths of the stone. "Unlike a traditional diamond that reflects light, a salt-and-pepper diamond pulls you in. Encourages a second look. The longer you look, the more you see."

He tried to reach out, to grasp a memory of the faceless red-haired woman. To summon an image of a woman he had apparently considered asking to be his wife.

An endless darkness thwarted his efforts. As if there was nothing beyond the past few hours. Suddenly angry, he tried harder, focused more, demanded his body release whatever it was concealing from him.

Searing pain shot through his head. His eyes scrunched shut as he suppressed a groan.

"Mr. Adamos?"

"A moment," he ground out.

Finally, the pain passed. When it did, he opened his eyes to see a bottle of water in front of him and Miss Smythe watching him.

"Once you're recovered, you have five minutes to tell me what's going on or leave."

He breathed in deeply, took a long drink of water and then sat back.

"A headache, Miss Smythe. Surely, you've heard of them."

Her eyes narrowed as she sat back.

"While I may interact with clients from a variety of backgrounds, if you're indulging in any illicit substance, I'll have you—"

"Strike that thought from your mind."

The authoritative command flowed naturally from his tongue. To her credit, Miss Smythe didn't flinch even as she gave him the tiniest of contrite nods.

"My apologies if I have offended you. But," she countered, leaning forward and crossing her arms so they gently pressed her breasts up, "you're still not telling me the truth."

"You're a beautiful woman, Miss Smythe. But it will take more than a little cleavage to have me reveal my secrets."

She let out a chuckle and leaned back into her chair.

"Worth a try." She sobered. "Mr. Adamos, to date our dealings have been nothing but professional. You paid on time, and in full. Your requests for the ring were obviously well-thought-out and detailed. But I have been in business long enough to know that something has changed since our last parting. Perhaps it is personal, and if so, I will drop the topic. But if it affects your purchase, or my company, I have a right to know."

He stared at her for a long moment. It would be taking a risk, an early one. Revealing his secret went against an instinct imprinted so deeply inside him he didn't question it. But he also recognized that, so far, this was the only link he had.

"I woke up an hour ago with no memory of who I am."

It gave him a small jolt of satisfaction to see her mouth drop open.

"Excuse me?"

"I woke up in a suite in The Bancroft an hour ago. I had a splitting headache and my chest felt like it was on fire. I have no memory of who I am, no wallet, no phone," he held up his left hand, "and no watch. All I could find, besides some very expensive luggage and an envelope full of euros, was your business card."

Her eyes darted between him and the ring box, now closed and pushed off to the side. "No memories at all? Not of your initial appointment five days ago?"

He waited a moment, let his eyes roam around the room. It felt familiar, but aside from the brief flashes he'd experienced outside when he'd first arrived, nothing else appeared.

"A flash here and there. Nothing substantial."

"Why not go to the police? The hospital?"

"Those routes will take time. When I confirmed today's date and time, I decided that coming here would offer me the quickest route to the question of who I am."

She tapped a manicured finger on the desk. Once, then once again, the sound echoing in the room. He maintained her gaze, accepting her assessment yet not backing down.

At last, she leaned back into her chair.

"The name you provided was John Adamos."

"A name I don't recognize."

She shrugged. "I wouldn't be surprised if it was a fake. Smythe's has been in business for generations. We thrive on exclusivity and mystery. Part of that includes not asking details of our clients. If they have a card, they get admitted. If they have money, we accept their order. Beyond that, we know very little about the people we work for."

He stood and began to pace. "When did I make the appointment?"

"Three weeks ago, when you submitted a request and the deposit."

"Deposit?"

"I require half, but you paid in full. One million euros."

He stared at her. "A million?"

"Yes." She shrugged a bare shoulder. "We're the best."

"And I said nothing about the woman this ring is for?"

Something wistful passed across Miss Smythe's face, so quickly John would have missed it if he hadn't been watching her carefully.

"No." She leaned forward. "But I've been in this showroom since I was a child. First watching my father, then learning, then leading. I know the difference between clients who want to impress someone, clients who are desperate, clients who are here simply for the thrill."

"The thrill?"

"Smythe's is by referral only to the world's elite. The art you saw on the ground floor serves as an excuse for the people who come to our door should anyone ask questions. A private collection that only the most esteemed art lovers are granted access to." The same proud smile he'd glimpsed earlier returned. "Without the black card you had in your possession, probably given to you by a former client, you would have either been turned away by Henry or one of the other guards." She smirked. "It's incredible how many politicians, movie stars and royals will pay hundreds of thousands just so they can engage in a clandestine appointment and own a piece of jewelry from my shop."

His lips quirked. "Did I present as a spoiled bastard?"

The smirk faded. "No." Miss Smythe opened the box and gazed at the ring. This time there was no mistaking the sadness in her eyes. "No, whoever you purchased this for is a fortunate woman to have someone who cares about her so deeply. You declined champagne. You booked an hour and took great care in examining the jewels. Many come to me wanting the most expensive or exclusive. You wanted something that, as you told me, would be beautiful but unique, enigmatic." Another smile flashed, genuine and nostalgic. "This ring was one I greatly enjoyed working on."

That sense of urgency invaded once more.

"Is there anything else you can tell me?"

"You set your appointment for two weeks out. You came in last week, picked out this diamond," she said with a nod to the box, "and arranged to come back today to pick up the ring."

"And I left no contact information? No phone, no email?"

Her fingers danced across the screen of her computer.

"You left an address." She rattled off the numbers and name of a street. "It's on the island of Grenada in the Caribbean Sea, care of Esmerelda Clark."

Esmerelda. The name rushed through him. He knew the name. Could see full lips turned up in a rare smile, green eyes dotted with gold and sparkling with laughter, red curls framing a freckled face.

"Do you know who she is?"

"No. As I mentioned, we honor our clients' wishes for privacy and do not conduct any background checks."

He steeled himself against the sudden frenetic energy that urged him to get up, to find Esmerelda Clark, to do *something.* He would find her. He had to find her. Surely, he wouldn't have put down the name of some random woman for such an important transaction. At the very least, she would probably have some answers about who he was.

But something innate told him that Esmerelda Clark wasn't just a resource. No, she was important. Perhaps even the woman he had planned to present this ring to.

"Will you write down the address for me?"

"Yes."

Miss Smythe jotted down the address on a piece of paper and handed it to him.

"I do have a request, Mr. Adamos."

"You've given me answers." He picked up the box. "And an invaluable ring. Name it and it's done."

Her lips tilted up.

"Call and tell me how the story ends."

CHAPTER TWO

To ANYONE WALKING by on the white sands of Little Cove Beach, the woman lounging in the hammock was enjoying her vacation. Sun filtered through the palm trees and warmed her skin. A gentle breeze drifted in off the cerulean blue waves, carrying the crisp, salty scent of the Caribbean Sea. A glass of Grenadian rum punch sat within reach on the ground, droplets of condensation dripping lazily down onto the sand.

Esme Clark sighed. It was hard to enjoy her vacation when, just over a month ago, she'd been fired by her former boss and ex-lover. That her dismissal had been delivered so coldly by the man who just a week before had made love to her during a magical night in Paris had made it all the more humiliating.

Sex, she reminded herself grimly. *We had sex. That's it.*

For a moment, she'd actually imagined herself in love with her boss. She'd known nothing could come of it. He was a prince. The heir to the throne of a small island nation off the coast of Portugal that had done surprisingly well for itself in recent times. Despite the occasional sweet story in the news or the romance novels she liked to read in bed late at night, reality was far crueler. Princes did not marry their bodyguards.

But for the first time in her life, even knowing how it would have to end, she had thrown caution to the wind and succumbed to her own desires. Desires that had been haunting her for the past year ever since she'd been injured protecting Prince Julius during a parade. She'd tried to rise when he'd visited her in the hospital. He'd gently pushed her back, sat by her bedside and chatted with her, even gifted her a copy of one of her favorite books. He'd made her laugh. When she'd looked at him, she'd seen a spark in his eyes, an awareness of her as a woman.

For months, she'd resisted indulging in anything physical. Too bad the same couldn't be said for her emotions. Something had changed between them after that morning in the hospital. It had been small things at first, like him showing up at her physical therapy appointment to see how she was progressing. She had assured herself it was something he would have done for any one of his security detail who had suffered an injury in the line of duty. For all the whisperings of the prince's cold and transactional way of handling his role, he invested in his people.

Except it had been something more. She'd resisted the pull between them for more than a year, the heated glances, the deep curve of his smile when they were alone.

Until Paris. Until one night when she had finally given in. They'd slept together—to think of it in any other terms but that was to invite heartache—followed less than a week later by his summoning her to his office where he'd informed her that he would be looking for a fiancée at the direction of his father, the king. Icy fingers wrapped around her heart still as she remembered staring at him, trying to keep her mouth from dropping open. She'd known when she'd gone to bed with him that it would be a short-term affair at most. What she hadn't expected were the emotions that had stirred: jealousy, hurt, loss.

And then he'd added fury to the volatile churn of feelings inside her chest by saying, in the coldest of voices, that given the circumstances it would be better if she was reassigned.

"It's over, Miss Clark. It has been since Paris."

Anger surged through her. She momentarily embraced it, savored the flash of fire in her veins. Anger was powerful. Anger yanked her away from the dark pit of sadness and self-pity.

And from desire. She kept it buried more often than not. But there were still moments, especially at night, when it would slide through her body, dipping into her dreams and stirring heated recollections of the way he'd slid her shirt from her shoulders, trailing his lips down the back of her neck and over the curve of her shoulder as his hands had cupped her breasts—

Stop. She'd mistaken seduction for tenderness, sex for lovemaking. Yes, Julius had been the best lover she'd been with. *So far,* she reminded herself firmly. *The best lover so far.* While she couldn't even begin to entertain the possibility of sex or a relationship right now, telling herself that she would move on helped.

That and the anger. The anger helped most of all.

Fortunately, she'd managed to harness some anger that day. It had kept the tears at bay and strengthened her voice as she'd simply bowed her head, replied "Yes, Your Highness," and savored the satisfying flare of shock in his eyes before she'd turned and walked out.

Instead of reporting to the Royal Security Office, where she would have had to face her coworkers and her father, the head of the royal family's security team, she had gone straight to her apartment in the wing reserved for palace employees. She'd packed up her few belongings, booked a ticket to Scotland and typed up a resignation letter in less than an hour. She'd hit send on the email as she'd arrived at the airport. Her father had called less than five minutes later, and had been calling almost every day since.

Once she would have been grateful for his attention. But it wasn't a personal interest in her. No, it was his concern for the effect her abrupt departure could have on his career that spurred his calls. Not her. Never her.

She'd sent every call to voice mail.

A sigh escaped her lips. She stared up through the fronds of the palm tree as the anger seeped out. Pain trickled in through the cracks in her heart, spreading and weighing her down until she felt so heavy she couldn't move.

Was there something fundamentally wrong with her? Was she destined to go her whole life being unwanted? Her mother had divorced her father and moved back to Scotland when Esme had been ten, then across the ocean to New York to follow a surgeon who had swept her off her feet when Esme was thirteen. Esme's father had been more focused on steadily climbing the ranks from palace gate guard to head of the entire royal family's security. Neither of them had cared much for being parents or the daughter they had created.

Their indifference had hardened her. She'd never allowed herself to be vulnerable again, including the few men she'd dated over the years, two of whom she'd allowed the intimacy of sharing her bed. None of them had been granted access to her heart.

Until Julius. Until he'd looked at her like he'd really seen her and slid past her defenses.

She sat up with a frustrated huff and maneuvered out

of the hammock. Why on earth was she wasting time ruminating on the past and the people who had deserted her time and again? She was in Grenada, for God's sake, on the first vacation she'd ever taken. Yes, her heart was still broken. Yes, when she closed her eyes at night she still saw Julius's face, heard him whisper her name in the dark as he'd loved her body and brought her to heights of passion she had never imagined possible.

And yes, when she thought of how cold he'd looked when he'd told her she was being reassigned, how nonchalantly he'd delivered the news of his upcoming engagement, she felt as if someone had punched her in the stomach and left her gasping for breath.

But each day away from the most agonizing moment of her life was a step toward her future. The one good thing to come out of her and Julius's tryst was their walk through Paris hours before they'd finally given in to their shared desires. He'd mentioned seeing her at a café the day before, how relaxed she'd looked.

"I felt like I was seeing the real you for the first time."

"I don't even know who the real me is."

The honesty of her statement surprised them both. Sadness twisted in her chest. How awful to go twenty-six years of one's life and realize you had lived it in pursuit of things others wanted for you.

"Look at me."

She did, struck once more by her body's sensual response to him, a response made even more potent by the rare smile on his full lips. He looked at her with something more than just simple desire. Something that both seduced and frightened her.

"Perhaps there are parts of yourself yet to be revealed. But the Esmerelda Clark I know is an incredible woman."

She'd believed every word. Every single calculated, flowery bit of sycophancy he'd delivered with confident charm.

She swallowed past the lump in her throat and latched onto the positive that had come out of their exchange. She had lived so much of her life for others. Never for herself.

Boarding the plane and watching Rodina fade to a tiny emerald speck on the blue waters of the Atlantic had twisted her battered and bruised heart into a hard knot. She loved her country. The rolling hills offset by towering oak forests, the black sand beaches that gently faded into the ocean, and the towering mountains at the southern end of the country, always capped by snow, had been like living in a fairy tale. Yet the country had its practical side, too. They mirrored their neighbor to the east, Portugal, with their massive olive tree groves and wheat fields. Manufacturing had also steadily grown under the guidance of Julius's father.

She hadn't just loved her country. She'd been proud of it. It was why, when her father had pushed her to go through the academy to become a part of the royal's security team, she'd agreed. She hadn't quite known what to do with herself after graduating from university. And yes, part of her had hoped to please him. But she'd also been proud to serve Rodina, and proud of herself when she'd been assigned to Prince Julius Carvalho's security detail just six months after she'd graduated.

Julius's attempt at reassigning her had nearly killed her. He'd phrased it as a promotion, becoming the leader of his cousin Vera's security team instead of serving as a "simple guard" on his. But she'd seen the reassignment for what it was; an attempt to make a problem disappear. Vera was kind but served in more of a ceremonial role. The girl was young and preferred events like charity luncheons versus trips overseas to meet with leaders on economic issues. Leadership position or not, Esme's days would have been boring, lifeless. A punishment for allowing the one man she never should have fallen for into her heart.

Yet Julius's banishment had also set her free. For the first time in her life, she had no father pushing her to pursue the career he'd always envisioned for the son he'd never had. No mother whose distant elegance had caught Esme in the middle of trying to be the child her father had wanted while striving to be a cultured, well-behaved lady like her mother desired.

She missed Rodina. One day she would return. But she needed to figure out who she was first.

She stretched her arms up to the sky, then leaned down, picked up her cocktail and took a long, leisurely sip. The sweet, tart flavors of orange and pineapple juice mixed pleasantly with the rum. Waves lapped against the beach. The breeze stirred the fronds of the palm trees and created a shushing sound that teased the stress from her shoulders.

After another drink, she let the diaphanous robe she'd picked up at a beachside shop slip from her shoulders onto the sand and moved down the beach. The rum flowed warmly through her veins as she walked into the ocean. Hills covered in palm trees and orchids cradled the cove before sloping gently down into the water.

She had another three weeks in paradise. Living in the palace apartments reserved for staff and having no social life had left her with a comfortable savings account. She would enjoy her time here. And when that time was up, she would move on. She'd overcome rejection before. She would do so again.

With confidence and determination banishing the

remnants of her pity party, she moved deeper until water splashed gently against her waist. She sank down, let the ocean close over her head and drifted for a moment in the shallows; blissfully alone, weightless. For the first time in a month, she felt at peace.

She released a breath, let herself sink lower. The swimming survival course had been her favorite part of academy training. It had been one of the rare times she'd let her mind stray and indulged in the fantasy of floating in the ocean on some faraway beach.

Her lips curved up in a smile even as her lungs started to tighten. Perhaps she could get certified in scuba diving, or book a snorkeling excursion...

Awareness pricked the back of her neck as she heard a dim splash. Before she could surface, thick arms wrapped around her body and hauled her out of the water.

Panic pierced her for a brief moment. There was no backup, no button she could push, no phone number she could call.

All she had was herself.

Her training kicked in. She let her body go limp. The man swore as they pitched forward. His grip tightened for a moment, but as they hit the water his hold loosened. She pushed away from him and shot up. As soon as her feet hit the sand, she swiped the water from her eyes and spun. The man faced away from her and was getting to his feet. She lunged, wrapping one around his neck and grabbing the back of his head with her other hand as she pushed him down onto his knees.

Exhilaration pumped through her.

"Why did you attack me?"

"I thought you were drowning."

She froze.

No. It can't be.

Her hold loosened. He stood in one fluid motion, breaking her grip as he turned and wrapped his arms around her, pinning her arms to her sides.

She blinked rapidly, her mind trying to accept the reality of what she was seeing.

"Julius?"

He smiled down at her, and her damned body responded, flutters dancing in her belly as heat crept up her neck.

"Of all the welcomes I've imagined on my trip here, I can safely say that was not one of them."

CHAPTER THREE

HIS HANDSOMENESS HIT her hard, just like it had the first time she'd laid eyes on him at the academy. The broad forehead and sharp cheekbones, offset by full, sensual lips, were all familiar. But the thickness of his beard and the longer cut of his hair, now hanging in wet strands turned to dark gold, sharply contrasted with the brooding air the so-called "Ice Prince" had exuded back home.

She breathed in, an action she quickly regretted as her breasts pressed more fully against his chest. Between the barely-there coverage of her bikini top and his ocean-soaked T-shirt, she could feel the heat of his skin against hers, the hardened muscle. Memories stirred of the night they'd lain together in bed, naked bodies entwined, the intimacy of lying together almost as powerful as when they'd joined.

Stop! She had to get a grip. Yes, they'd had an incredible night together. But the relationship she'd created in her mind, one of mutual respect and a desire to support the country they both loved, one deepened by the knowledge that she might have been called on at any moment to surrender her life for his, had been nothing more than a fantasy.

"It was one night, Miss Clark," he said with such dis-

dain she wanted to curl inside herself and hide from the
shame his words birthed. "But with my now impending
marriage, it's best if you're reassigned elsewhere."

Cold. Callous. Everything she'd heard whispered about
him had been true.

Anger started to churn in her belly, rising up and twin-
ing through her veins with a fiery strength that eclipsed
her heartache and humiliation.

"Why on earth would you think I was drowning?" she
asked, keeping her voice neutral. "You know the survival
course requires being submerged for at least two minutes."

His brow furrowed. One hand came up to push the hair
out of his eyes. "I—"

She swept her arms up and broke his grasp. Planting
both hands on his chest, she gave him a shove and was re-
warded with the sight of the prince falling back into the
ocean. She savored the sight of him tumbling beneath the
waves before making a beeline for the beach.

The sound of Julius cursing behind her made her smile.
She spared a glance over her shoulder and grinned when
she saw the thunderous expression on his face.

"What the devil was that for?" he shouted.

She froze. The anger paused, then seethed, churned,
burning into white-hot rage as she slowly turned to face
him.

"You can't be serious."

He stared at her for a long moment, then looked down
as he let out a frustrated sigh.

"Look, Miss Clark. Esme—"

"No." Her voice rang out over the waves. "You ad-
dressed me as 'Miss Clark' the day you fired me. You don't
have permission to address me by my first name. Ever."

He scrubbed a hand over his face, then started walking

out of the waves. She stood her ground and did her best to ignore the way his shirt molded to his muscled chest, the wet cloth revealing the dark golden hair that trailed down his stomach and disappeared beneath the waistband of his pants.

He stalked up onto the sand. With every step closer he took, her heart upped its rhythm, until it was beating so fast it was a wonder she didn't pass out.

"Miss Clark, we have to talk."

Her traitorous heart leapt. She mentally snatched it, pushed her treacherous emotions away.

"If you're offering to hire me back, the answer is—"

"Would you just listen to me, damn it?"

Something in his tone slipped past her hurt. She waited a moment, two, then evaluated the man before her. The man who looked more like a tourist on vacation than a royal prince. The man who had easily lost ten pounds since she'd last seen him and now sported a cut on one cheek. The man who was looking at her with a touch of uncertainty in his amber eyes.

She'd cut off all ties to the palace when she'd left. Told the few acquaintances she had that she would be in touch soon with no real intention of actually following through. She'd also avoided the media, not wanting to see carefully curated photos of Julius with whatever princess or duchess or heiress his father had picked as the perfect wife.

Something had obviously happened since she'd left. Her heart pounded once, twice, her hands yearning to reach out and smooth the furrow between his brows. To wrap her arms around him just once more the way she had the morning after they'd made love. He'd been standing at the balcony doors, hands tucked in his pockets, shoulders rigid as if he'd already resumed carrying the weight of the world. She'd walked up behind him, laid one hand on his back. The muscles had tensed beneath her touch. Reality had told her to step back, give him space. The intimacy they'd shared last night and into the early hours of the morning encouraged otherwise. So she'd slowly slid her arms around his waist, laid her cheek against his shoulder blade. And when he'd finally released a breath, relaxing in her hold, accepting the strength she offered for whatever battle he was fighting, she'd tipped over the edge she'd avoided for so long.

An edge she found once again as he watched her, his eyes roaming over her face as if he'd never seen her before.

"It's over, Miss Clark."

Her chin rose, her spine straightening as she faced down her former lover.

"I'm done listening to you." She executed a formal bow. "Your Highness." And then she turned, swept up her robe and walked away, leaving a soaking wet prince alone on the beach.

John stared after Esme until she disappeared up the winding wood stairs that led from the beach up to the tiny cottage perched on a cliff. He turned away and swore.

That could have gone better.

He'd gone to the cottage as soon as his plane had landed. The taxi had zipped past elegant resorts shrouded behind massive shrubs, colorful homes and the turquoise waters of the Caribbean Sea.

He'd seen it, registered it. But his thoughts had been solely focused on finding the mysterious Esmerelda Clark.

Which is why when he'd knocked, then knocked harder still and finally peered in the windows, he hadn't been able to stop the string of curse words that had tumbled from his lips. To come so far and find the cottage empty had left him trembling with anger and a gnawing fear that the woman who might hold all the answers was gone.

He'd spied the stairs curling down from the back porch. Instinct had nudged him to walk down the winding staircase that descended down the cliff before leveling out into a narrow boardwalk across a stream, then several more steps down onto a yellow-white sandy beach.

And then he'd seen her. Standing on the sand in a bikini that left little of her lithe, toned body to the imagination, hair spilling down her back in flaming red-gold curls. His anger and fear had evaporated in a moment. She was here. She was here and she was familiar in a way that he couldn't explain. He didn't know her middle name or what flowers she liked or what their relationship had been like before he'd ended up in London.

But he knew her. Knew her, craved her with not just his body but a need that surpassed the mere physical.

When she'd walked into the water, he'd held back, pulling himself back together piece by piece so that when he moved onto the beach, he wouldn't frighten her.

Except then she'd slipped beneath the waves and hadn't come back up.

He'd waited. But the seconds had stretched. He'd walked onto the beach, spied her red hair below the surface. When the seconds had turned into a minute and she hadn't moved, fear had propelled him into the water.

He rubbed his neck. The woman had a grip. And a grudge. The impressions that flirted with the edges of his broken mind had led him to the assumption that he and Esmerelda had been lovers. An assumption he thought confirmed by the brief flare of desire in her eyes when he'd held her nearly naked body close. A desire that had kindled an answering fire deep within him.

But she hadn't said anything about a romantic connection. No, she'd referenced working for him and tossed in that odd bow at the end. Had they been coworkers, or he'd been her boss, and tried to take the relationship from professional to intimate? Worse, had he crossed a line?

The headache returned with a vengeance and pounded at his temples. He'd obviously done something to taint whatever relationship they'd had. To make her walk away without a backward glance.

Ridiculous for the rejection of a woman he couldn't even remember to hurt. Yet hurt it did, a crackling pain beneath his skin coupled with an emptiness in his chest that rivaled the emptiness inside his head.

Enough.

He'd come this far, spent most of his money to find Esmerelda Clark. He would atone for whatever atrocities he'd committed in his murky past. But right now, he needed answers.

Five minutes later he stood outside the door of the cabin. He forced himself to not fling the door open and seek her out. As he raised his fist to knock, the door swung open. Esmerelda stood framed in the doorway, her eyes snapping green fire and her hair caught up in a loose bun at the nape of her neck. She'd pulled a blue T-shirt on but had yet to pull on shorts, leaving her long legs bare to his gaze.

"Did you get seawater in your ears?"

"Excuse me?"

"I said no."

She started to close the door. John flung up his arm and braced it against the door. Her eyes widened.

And then she got angry. She drew herself up to her full

five-foot-five, her body tightening and shifting like a snake getting in position to strike.

She was glorious.

"If you are even contemplating forcing yourself in here, sir, I will break every bone in your body, starting with your—"

"I need your help."

She paused.

"Please," he added.

He knew the moment it worked because she slowly uncoiled, her body loosening, her stance relaxing a fraction as she regarded him with curiosity and suspicion.

"With what?"

He hesitated. Where to begin? He'd obviously done something to her in his previous life. Hurt her somehow.

Her eyes narrowed. She started to push the door shut. He had to plant himself to keep her sudden shove from knocking him off balance.

"I don't know who I am."

She stopped. Her eyes moved over his face.

His relief at sharing his predicament proved short-lived.

"Look, I can't help you." She glanced away, the first time she had done so, as if it made her uncomfortable to look at him. "I understand you're under a tremendous amount of pressure, not to mention the engagement—"

Disappointment speared his chest.

"We're not engaged?"

A stricken look passed over her face, pain flashing in her eyes as her lips parted in shock. He swallowed past the sudden thickness in his own throat.

"How can you even ask that?"

"Esme… Miss Clark," he amended as her lips thinned. "When I say I don't know who I am, I mean that literally."

Silence descended between them, thick and heavy. Dimly he heard the distant roar of the surf, the melancholy coo of a nearby bird, the thudding of his own heart. She stared at him, as if waiting for him to break character, to laugh and say it was all a joke.

"If this is some sort of scheme or manipulation—"

He reached down and grabbed her hand, ignoring her gasp and the electric awareness that surged up his arm. He leaned down and pressed her hand against the wound at the base of his skull. The initial touch made him bite back a hiss of pain. Her fingers tensed then gentled, tracing the swelling with a touch so soft it calmed some of the turmoil that had been churning inside him for the past twenty-four hours. As she leaned closer, he breathed in, smelling the salty scent of the sea clinging to her skin. Sea and something else…something floral and feminine that made him want to drag her against him and bury his face in her hair.

Mine.

The word shot through him, awoke something lodged deep in his chest. A possessiveness that felt right even as it unsettled him, to have such strong emotions for a woman he couldn't remember anything about.

"Turn around."

He kept his surprise at her sudden brusque demeanor hidden and followed her direction. Even though his mind resisted taking orders, took umbrage at being talked to like that, he forced himself to be vulnerable, to surrender something of himself.

"Crouch down, please. Sir," she added.

"You worked for me?" he asked as her fingers probed the wound once more, her touch now efficient.

"I did."

"What happened?"

"You fired me."

The words were said plainly, factually. It didn't mask the hurt lingering in her voice, the shade of embarrassment.

Before he could ask for details, she spoke.

"What's the last thing you remember?"

"Waking up in my hotel room yesterday afternoon."

"Blunt force trauma to the base of your skull." She walked around him and looked in his eyes. "Pupils appear normal. Any vomiting, dizziness?"

"No. Some nausea when I first awoke, but it disappeared quick enough."

"What did the doctor say?"

"Doctor?"

Her eyes widened before narrowing to tiny slits as she planted her fists on her hips. The gesture made her look like an adorably pissed-off fairy.

"You did go to a hospital, didn't you?"

An ache started to build in his temples as he straightened to his full height. Instead of stepping back or showing any sign of hesitancy, she merely lifted her chin and met his gaze head-on.

Oh, yes. He liked this woman very much.

"A hospital would have taken time. I was given your name and address and came straight here?"

She frowned. "Got my name from who?"

He held up his hand.

"Before I answer any more questions, tell me…"

He paused. Physically steeled himself for whatever response he was about to receive.

"Who am I?"

One hand came up, her fingers rubbing at her forehead. She muttered under her breath in a language he knew— Portuguese—and then looked up at him.

"Sit down. Please," she added huffily when he arched a brow at her command. "I'll be right back."

He moved to the table and chairs set at the far end of the porch that ran the length of the cottage. The chair let out a protesting groan as he sat. Given the hints of rust poorly disguised by a thin layer of white paint, it was a miracle the chair had lasted as long as it had.

Esme appeared a moment later, clad in the wet shirt that clung to her body and a pair of shorts, two steaming mugs in her hands. She set one in front of him as she sat in the chair across from him.

"Spiced coffee."

Cinnamon and a touch of sweetness swirled on his tongue as he took a long drink. The hot liquid warmed his throat, gave himself something tangible to focus on.

"Thank you." He set his cup down. "John Adamos isn't my real name, is it?"

"Why do you ask?"

"It doesn't feel like my name. There's no recognition, no connection."

"No. It's not your real name." Her gaze flicked down to her own cup, then back up to his. A veil had dropped over her eyes. The woman in front of him was even more of a stranger than the one he had happened on down on the beach. Cool, collected.

Withdrawn.

"Your name is Julius Carvalho."

Something flickered inside him, a flame of recognition. Distant, but there.

"Julius," he repeated.

"Yes." She breathed in deeply. "Crown Prince Julius Adamos Carvalho."

Silence stretched between them once more. Laughter

died in his throat when she didn't smile, didn't chuckle, simply watched him with that clinical gaze.

"Prince," he echoed.

"Yes. Heir to the throne of the island nation of Rodina."

CHAPTER FOUR

JULIUS HADN'T MOVED from the chair in over thirty minutes. For the first minute after her pronouncement, he'd simply sat, as if absorbing the enormity of what she'd shared. Then he'd asked questions, collecting information about his life as if he were preparing to study for an exam. Every now and then he would pause, breathe in deeply, then continue. It was the only sign that the conversation was taxing him.

The more he'd talked, the more she'd recognized that this wasn't a ruse. A realization that had opened the door to fear that curled around her heart and crawled up her throat. Fear at whatever horrid thing had happened to him in London and caused this.

He'd resisted contacting the palace, saying he needed time to process what she'd shared. It had taken nearly ten minutes to convince him to let her call her friend Burak, a fellow guard who had been promoted to the head of Julius's detail after she'd left, and see if she could ferret out any information. Burak had grudgingly admitted that Julius had taken a sabbatical.

"Only a select few know his exact location. He made the private security I hired at the airport and threatened to fire me if I didn't pull them."

"So you're just letting the heir to the throne wander around the world?" Esme asked incredulously.

"He checks in every forty-eight hours by cell."

The edge in Burak's voice had made her change topics. She liked Burak, counted him as one of a tiny group of friends. Even if she strongly disagreed with how Julius had been allowed to roam free, she knew firsthand how the man operated. If he had decided on something, the only person he would ever bow to would be his father. And even then, if he believed in it strongly enough, he would put up one hell of a fight. It had been one of the qualities that had made her admire him even as she wanted to wring his neck.

Just like now. From here she could see the bruise just below his hairline, red turning to a mottled purple. The ugly scarlet of the cut on his face. What had he gotten into that he would have sustained such injuries?

She turned away from the window, not wanting him to suddenly turn and see her watching him like a mother hen. She put the used coffee mugs in the sink, rinsed them out, focused on the cold splash of water on her fingers, the smoothness of the porcelain in her hands, the slight clunking in the pipes.

Focus on the tangible.

Julius's voice echoed in her head. He'd come into her hospital room shortly after the accident. She'd been rising up from the depths of a nightmare, one filled with the screams of people and a frightened horse as searing pain burned through her skin. He'd taken her hand, his fingers rubbing soothing circles on her skin, as he'd told her to focus on the things she saw in her room, the things she heard. A simple exercise, but one that had grounded her and given her time to collect herself.

Perhaps that had been the moment she'd started to slip from respect into love.

She placed the mugs in the drying rack. Her hands rested on the edge of the countertop, then curled around the edge, a death grip as she bowed her head and blew out a harsh breath.

Deus me ajude.

She still loved him. After everything that had happened, love still beat inside her for a man who had used and betrayed her.

This can't be love.

Infatuation? A fantasy? The longings of a woman who had been rejected her whole life?

She grabbed onto that last thought. Of course it was hard to let go. She and Julius had grown close over the past year. He'd been there for her during her recovery, the grueling hours of physical therapy. He'd also been the first man she'd gone to bed with in over two years. It was only natural that she would still have lingering emotions, that she would feel upset that someone she had respected and come to care about had been hurt to the point of forgetting his entire life.

Upset and torn. Should she tell him about what they'd shared in Paris? Reliving the humiliation of those last few moments in his office before she'd walked out, convinced she'd never see him again?

Except what would that accomplish, other than further complicating their current situation? It wasn't as if they'd dated or had anything beyond that one night.

Get it together, Esmerelda.

The heir to the throne was sitting on her porch with no memory of who he was or what had happened to him. Now was not the time to struggle with unrequited emotions. No, she needed to get him back home to Rodina and into the care of a qualified physician since the foolish man had taken the address from that London jeweler and used almost all his cash to pay for a seat on a cargo plane that hadn't bothered to ask for a passport. When he'd told her that lovely tidbit, she'd had a vivid and painful image of him strapped into the back of a hold crowded with boxes of contraband as a rickety plane spiraled into the ocean.

If she suppressed that horrifying vision and instead focused on the reality that the so-called "Ice Prince" of Rodina had flown on a cargo plane with a bag of cash with a million-euro ring secreted in the bottom, it was almost amusing.

The ring.

Just thinking about it sobered her instantly. She hadn't seen it yet. She had no wish to. Just the thought of it made her stomach roll.

"I can see the smoke coming out of your ears."

She froze, then silently swore. No one had snuck up on her in years. Slowly, she turned.

And realized that the house was far too tiny. How was it possible that a cottage that had seemed surprisingly roomy now seemed no bigger than a closet? He filled the space, all broad shoulders and lean muscle clad in the still-damp shirt and pants that, thankfully, had dried enough they no longer clung to his body.

"There's a lot to think about."

Thankfully her voice came out steadier than her chaotic stream of thoughts.

"Agreed." He glanced around the cottage, the casual gesture not masking the intensity in his eyes. "How did you find this place?"

"Vacation listing online."

Her jaw tightened as she followed his gaze. It wasn't the same caliber as the fancy Parisian hotel they'd made love in, or the sweeping glamor of the Rodinian seaside palace. Not even close, with the worn white wicker furniture and amateur photographs of Grenada on the faded blue walls.

But that had been part of its charm. It was clean, affordable and exactly the opposite of where she'd been living.

"Cozy."

"You mean cheap," she retorted.

Embarrassment crept up her neck as his gaze swung back to her, a slight smile tugging at one corner of his full lips. Lips she'd kissed, lips he'd used on her breasts, trailed over her stomach, then lower still to—

"Your blushes are telling."

"I don't blush." She moved to the living area and folded a blanket, needing something to do with her hands, to put distance between them. "I flush. There's a difference."

"Oh?"

"Blush implies roses, delicate pinks and beautiful women." She swallowed past the sudden lump in her throat. Beautiful women like her mother. Beautiful women like the future bride of Prince Julius Carvalho. "Flush is more accurate for someone like me."

"Someone like you?"

Surprised at the sudden hardening in his tone, she looked up to see him glowering at her.

"I turn red. Red underneath freckles, coupled with this hair, does not an attractive woman make."

"And who told you that?"

She laid the blanket on the sofa's sagging back and smoothed out the wrinkles. The sound of her mother's disappointed sigh when Esme had turned down yet another offer to have it professionally dyed to something "more suitable than that unfortunate mix of red and yellow," still sounded as piercing as it had the day her mother had said it.

On her thirteenth birthday.

"It doesn't matter." She'd told herself that so many times over the years until she'd almost believed it. "I don't know how we even got onto this ridiculous topic. We should be discussing what to do next with you and…all of this," she finished with a wave of her hand.

He inclined his head to her.

"Given you know more of…well, everything," he said with another faint smile, "I am at your mercy."

"All right." She sank down onto the arm of the sofa, details swirling through her mind. Her ability to analyze and create a plan was one of the few skills she felt truly confident in. That it was a part of her and not just something instilled on her by an aloof mother or a hard-nosed father.

"You should call the palace and let them know what happened to—"

"No."

Irritation trickled down her spine, but she kept it in check. She had conducted herself with the highest level of professionalism during her time as a guard.

Minus sleeping with the boss.

She silenced her conscience and returned his rigid expression with an impassive one of her own.

"I'm sorry, I must have misunderstood the part where you're at my mercy."

"If what you're telling me is true—"

"If?"

"You must admit, telling someone they're a prince and heir to a European nation is outlandish."

She cocked her head to one side and gave him a sweet smile.

"As outlandish as a prince showing up on the doorstep of the palace guard they fired from their service and claiming to have forgotten their entire life? Or perhaps as preposterous as said prince catching a cargo plane to—"

"Suficiente."

She didn't bother suppressing her smug smirk as he ran a frustrated hand through his hair.

He held up the prepaid cell phone he'd purchased at the airport.

"I found news stories to support what you told me."

Irritation flickered through her.

"I didn't lie."

"I know. Surely you can understand the need to see it with my own eyes, to catch up on…" He paused. "Well, my entire life. But," he added, stepping closer as he slid his hands into his pockets, "one thing was missing."

"What?"

"Any news on my engagement, the woman I'm dating, anything."

"Given that you hadn't dated anyone in over a year, I'm not surprised."

"Then I'm not engaged."

"Not yet. But you will be soon."

"To whom?"

"You didn't share with me. You may not have even known at the time who your fiancée was to be."

His lips parted. "How is that possible?"

"Because 'royal marriages are transactions for the betterment of the country.' A direct quote from both you and your father. I'm sure a list of recommended candidates was provided to you around the time or shortly after I left. You must have traveled to London to select a ring for her."

Jealousy coiled in her stomach, followed by shame. The woman chosen to be the future Queen of Rodina would have been someone she would have been proud to serve and protect. Up until she shirked everything she had vowed to uphold and slept with said woman's future husband.

He turned away, giving her a moment to blink back the hot sting of tears. He reached into the bag she'd brought inside while he'd ruminated on the porch after her incredible announcement and pulled out an obsidian-colored velvet box.

"You were listed as the primary contact for the ring. Why?"

She looked away from the box and out the window to the sea.

Focus on the future. Answer his questions. Get him help. Get him out of your life once and for all.

"It's standard practice to list a member of the security detail as the contact for any business a member of the royal family doesn't want the public knowing about."

"But you said you haven't worked for my security team for over a month."

"You must have made the appointment before you fired me."

"With an address in the Caribbean?"

That part stumped her. He'd most likely hired a detective, someone outside of the palace, to track her down. Why was anyone's guess.

And she didn't care. Couldn't care.

"Why did I fire you?"

It was too much. She'd lasted this long. But it was time for Julius to go. To return to his life and receive the care he needed from a doctor. To rejoin royal life and leave her behind.

"You'll either remember or someone else will inform you." She held out her phone. "You can use my cell to call in for your security check. Tell them what happened and they'll—"

"No."

Irritation flickered through her.

"I beg your pardon?"

"I just found out I'm a prince. A prince who is heir to the throne," he repeated, his voice dark and dangerous and hard. "What you just described sounds unappealing at best. My every move shadowed by a security team. An engagement to a woman selected like I'm shopping for produce at the damned market."

"What did you expect?" she snapped. "You're royalty. Real-life royalty. This isn't a fairy tale, Your Highness."

"Do you know what I expected, Esmerelda?"

She stifled the stirring deep in her belly at his use of her full name. The last time he'd said it, he'd moaned it against her lips as he'd slid inside her.

"I can only imagine, sir."

"I expected for you to be the woman I bought the ring for. That I would arrive here and find out I was a banker or a CEO, something mundane that would explain the massive amount of cash and the diamond." His eyes flashed as his fingers tightened around the box. "I thought this was for you, not some faceless woman chosen off of a list."

She tried to ignore the jab of the knife to her heart as he casually mentioned the possibility of having bought the ring for her. She'd known once they'd kissed, once she'd made the decision to finally share her body with him, that it couldn't last. That at most, it would never go beyond an affair. He was a prince. Princes married princesses, duchesses, politicians' daughters, other wealthy people who brought their own connections to the union. She'd known, and accepted, that there would be pain. To her, the year they'd spent together as prince and bodyguard, coming to know each other on a deeper level after her accident, followed by the most incredible night she'd ever spent with a man, had been worth the eventual heartache.

She just hadn't expected the end to come so soon, nor so viciously.

"It's not all glass slippers and champagne, sir. I'm sorry you had to find out this way, but I can't help you anymore. I'm sure a plane can be ready in an hour to take you home."

He stood, regarding her with an intensity that made her want to squirm. Would he suddenly remember? Would the memories come rushing back like they did in the movies, leaving her to experience his disgust and rejection all over again?

"I have impressions. Feelings. They're faint, almost as if a shadow has been wrapped around them."

He stepped closer. She stood her ground, willing herself not to retreat.

"But before I even heard your name, I remembered you." His hand came up, his fingers gliding across one of her wild curls. "When Miss Smythe named you as the contact, I knew that I knew you. That there's something important, something unfinished, with you."

Her heart cried out at the passion in his gaze. Her mind stifled the desire.

"Perhaps it's guilt for acting like a pompous jerk when you removed me from your detail."

His lips tightened.

"We were lovers."

"No."

The lie came quickly, uttered with such feeling she almost believed it herself. *Not a lie*, she reassured herself even as her conscience disagreed. He had never loved her.

He'd had his fun, then chosen to distance himself so he and his reputation wouldn't be sullied by a one-night stand with his bodyguard.

"No?" His thick brows drew together. "I remember…"

She nearly caved at the confusion on his face. Nearly told him about the night in Paris.

"I have a reputation to uphold, Miss Clark. Your continued employment on my security team threatens that."

"We were not lovers, Your Highness. I was your bodyguard. We were friends. Or at least I thought we were." She looked away then, knowing she was stretching the truth. But she couldn't bear this again, to rehash the horrible things he'd said and relive the heartache only to have him rush off again as soon as he regained his memory. "Your father requested you marry. You reassigned me without even talking to me about it beforehand and delivered the news rather brutally."

"Why?" he demanded.

"You said it would look better. Your new team was all male." She let the implication hang between them as she tugged on her robe and belted it tightly at the waist. "I declined the reassignment, walked out of the palace and hopped on a plane. I was tired of letting people in my life guide my choices. I stopped briefly at the home my mother left me in Scotland to oversee my things getting moved in, then booked a flight to Grenada to figure out what I wanted for my life. And now you're here."

She faced him then, shoulders thrown back, holding his intense gaze.

And nearly crumpled as he flipped the lid open on the ring box.

CHAPTER FIVE

SHE HAD NEVER cared for diamonds. To her they had always seemed bland. But this diamond, flecked with black and surrounded by blue gems and tiny pearls, entranced her, drew her into its depths.

A sunbeam fell on the diamond and made it glint. The flash of light made her wince, breaking the spell.

"Your future fiancée is a fortunate woman. Whoever she ends up being, I'm sure she'll appreciate it."

"And it was not for you? You're certain of that?"

She waited a moment, suppressing her anguish, her bitterness. When she spoke, she hoped he wouldn't detect the depth of strangled emotion in her voice.

"I can assure you that you would have never proposed to someone like me."

"Someone like you," he echoed with a frown as he thankfully snapped the box shut and placed it back on the table. "The second time you've used that phrase."

She nodded toward the box.

"The woman who will wear your ring will fit the part. Beautiful, distinguished, most likely wealthy, and with a family pedigree that traces back centuries." She held up her hand, wiggling her fingers. "Not a former bodyguard who's never had a manicure and drinks rum cocktails on a beach on a tiny island."

"You sound far more interesting than my future fiancée."

She brushed aside the hurt. To this man with no memory, she probably sounded fascinating. To Prince Julius Carvalho, the heir to Rodina's throne, she was nothing. He'd made that perfectly clear.

He circled around the sofa. Instinct told her to run. Training kept her in place as he drew near, filling every corner of the room with his dominating presence.

"Thank you, Your Highness."

The use of his title didn't stop his advance. Whatever had happened to cause his amnesia had certainly not dulled his powerful presence, his ability to command attention as soon as he walked into a room. It rippled off him, drew her in like a moth to a flame.

Except she wouldn't get burned. Not this time. She would not survive it if she did.

Julius stopped in front of her, less than a foot away, although it could have been less than an inch with the heat swirling between them. Their eyes met and the temperature rose.

"Whoever made you think you're not beautiful or fascinating or worthy was a fool."

"My mother."

"A fool," Julius repeated. "When I came to, I had three memories. One was of a voice. Another was a chandelier." He leaned forward a fraction, golden-brown eyes glinting. "The third was of your hair."

Her heart stuttered.

"My hair?"

"Yes." He reached out and twirled an errant curl around his finger. "Like flames spilling over my hands."

Longing pierced her heart like an arrow. Her own memories of that night rising unbidden from the depths of her mind. The depths she'd pushed them to to try and forget. Memories of him raising himself up on his arms after he'd kissed her. Long, drugging kisses that made her limbs heavy. The look in his eyes when he'd trailed his fingers through her hair had stirred something deeper than lust. For one moment, as he'd stroked the tresses and murmured *"Tão bonito,"* she'd felt truly beautiful for the first time in her life.

Remembering was too much. Too painful. He'd made her believe something that could never be true.

"Why would I have that memory if there was nothing between us?"

She paused, fumbled for a plausible excuse. Another memory surfaced, a lifeline. Something she could distract him with.

"I was in the hospital a year ago. You visited me. I had a head wound and you brushed back my hair to look at the bandage."

When he'd leaned down, devastatingly handsome in a steel-blue suit over a white dress shirt, and smoothed back errant curls from the white bandage plastered to her forehead, something had shifted inside of her. Respect had segued into longing, loyalty into longing. She'd tamped it for months, convinced it was one-sided and simply a product of the intimacy of laying down one's life for another.

Until Paris.

Suspicion flickered across his face.

"You believe that's what I'm remembering? Nothing else?"

"I don't know." She shrugged, strove for nonchalance as she forced herself to step away from him. The sheer magnetism of him was making her breathless. She needed room to breathe, to remember why she couldn't be the person he turned to in this hour of need.

She moved back toward the small kitchenette and set about making herself a cup of tea. "I have no idea what's going on inside your head, Your Highness, what memories are fact and what are fiction."

"I see."

Silence reigned behind her. She willed herself to stay strong, to not be the first to give in. The rest of the world rose up to fill the void, from the creaking of the roof to the shooshing of the breeze that lifted the faded gauze curtains hanging over the window. Each sound grew louder than the last. Pressure built in her chest, heavy and constricting, until she could barely breathe past the tightness in her throat.

"You need to check in with Burak, your head of security."

There. That was professional. And it started the ball rolling on getting him out of her cottage.

"Otherwise the armada will sail across the ocean to find me?"

"What is it you fear?" She turned and frowned at him. "You flew on a cargo plane to find me, to get answers. The palace could provide you with everything you're seeking. That and resources to help you heal."

"When I came to find you, there was one person I was focused on tracking down. Not an entire country that, as you described, looks to my father and me for leadership."

A small wrinkle appeared between his brows as he blinked twice. Subtle, but she knew the signs of an impending headache. How many times had she sat in his office at the end of a long day as they had debriefed, seen the tells that so many people missed? How many times in the past few months had she grown bolder, moving to make tea or offer him an aspirin?

"I need time, Esmerelda. Time to wrap my head around the enormity of what you've shared." He gave in then, the quickest touch of fingers to his temple. "Time to reconcile what I feel versus what you've told me. I will not be rushed."

Hope flared, bright and brilliant, then winked out just as quickly. It didn't matter if the desire that had brought them together was at the forefront of his mind. When he remembered, when he resumed his role back in Rodina, they would be right back where they had been five weeks ago. Hope was hopeless. It had no place here.

"When you do call Burak to check in, let him know you changed locations and that your wallet was stolen." She held out her hand for his phone, avoided touching his fingers as he passed it over. She plugged in Burak's number before she handed it back over. "They can have new identification, passport, credit cards and anything else you might need by tomorrow." She bit back a sigh. "You can stay here until they arrive."

She couldn't leave the heir to the Rodinian throne alone to fend for himself. The professional part of her knew that. Even if the personal part railed against it, instinctively knowing it wasn't a good idea.

The prince's eyes bored into hers.

"Are you sure?"

No.

"Yes. I'm not going to have your welfare on my conscience."

"Mercenary," he replied dryly. "But given that it benefits me, I won't argue." He glanced around the small cottage, the slightest lift to his brow. "Although I'm curious as to how two people will fit in such…intimate accommodations."

"There's a perfectly good couch in here. You can have the bed—"

"No."

Tension gripped her at his clipped tone.

"Excuse me?"

"I will not be taking your bed. Unless," he added with a quirk of his lips, "you're suggesting we share…"

Desire shot through her with such intensity she barely had the opportunity to conceal it. The idea of crowding onto the queen mattress with Julius's six-foot-three body stirred memories of how their limbs had become entwined during their second round of lovemaking. Every time she'd moved, it had been to feel the slide of her naked skin against his. The intimacy of her breasts pressed against the curling hair on his chest, her thighs shifting against his, his hands cupping her rear and pulling her closer against him, had been almost as dizzying as when he'd slid inside her the first time.

"That would hardly be appropriate. Especially," she added as much for his benefit as her own, "given that you have a ring and possibly a fiancée out there somewhere."

His face darkened.

"I am not taking your bed."

"Then sleep on the floor next to it. I'm not enjoying the comforts of a bed while the prince takes the couch."

Even though she had initially pursued her career at the encouragement of her father, out of some ridiculous need for his approval, the job had become ingrained in her. Fed by her genuine love and loyalty for her country, the thought of letting the prince she had sworn to protect with her life sleep on the couch nearly made her choke.

He stepped toward her.

"I will toss you into that bed if I have to."

His words lit the sensual tension hanging in the room. Eyes wide, Esme watched in stupefied fascination as his own gaze darkened, then swept over her from head to toe. She'd swapped out her bikini bottom for shorts when she'd come inside, but she might as well have been naked given the way Julius's eyes burned.

"What gives you the right to give me orders?"

"I'm a prince, aren't I?" A dangerous smile curved across his face, one that made her swallow hard. "Isn't giving orders part of what I do?"

"Yes. But you're no longer my prince." Suddenly furious, with both him and herself, she strode past him, deliberately letting her shoulder knock into his chest as she headed for the door. He had lost the right to tell her what to do. She wouldn't let anyone do that anymore. Not her father and certainly not Julius.

"Do what you want, *Julius*. Although I recommend calling Burak." She paused in the doorway and gave him an ornery smile. "Unless you want to test just how quickly the palace can track you down and haul your royal butt back to Rodina whether you like it or not."

With that parting shot, she let the door slam behind her.

CHAPTER SIX

"YES, BURAK, I assure you all is well. Thank you."

Julius hung up and sat back in the porch chair, closing his eyes against the pain exploding in his head. His captain of security had been suspicious. But the code word Esmerelda had included when she'd inputted Burak's contact information into his new phone had reassured the man. Burak had been less than happy about Julius's sudden jaunt to Grenada and suspicious of Julius's story that his personal bag with his passport and wallet had been stolen. The one thing that had placated him was that Julius was on a much smaller island with far fewer people than England.

He'd liked Burak. The man had balanced respect with backbone, the soft melody of a Turkish accent lacing his firm voice. He'd also been incredibly efficient at organizing several of Julius's requests.

But there had been no sense of knowing, no connection to the man who had been a part of his security detail for over a year. Not like there had been with Esmerelda. They'd discussed details like getting him access to his finances and a new passport. It had been a productive conversation. But it had also prodded the always present headache, spreading from an obscure ache at the base of his skull to his temples where it pounded away with reckless abandon.

Further evidence that he needed time. Time to rest, recuperate, hopefully remember more before he assumed the role of heir to an entire country.

Although it wasn't just that. After Esmerelda's revelation, she'd disappeared inside, which had given him time to absorb the magnitude of what she'd shared. He'd read up on himself, scrolling through photo after photo of him in elegant suits looking pensive, cold, shrewd. The few pictures of him with any women were over eighteen months old. Plenty of articles had speculated on ambassadors he had spoken with at dinners, daughters of wealthy business leaders whose hands he had held onto "a moment longer than others."

But there had been nothing that had given insight into who he was as a man. No hobbies, no candid photos, not even a smile. The lack of information, and the absence of any defining personality, had stoked the disquiet that had first appeared when he'd looked in the mirror and not recognized the face staring back at him.

Time. He needed time. He had confirmed with Burak that he would be gone the remaining two weeks they had previously agreed to. Two weeks to rest, to perhaps regain his memory.

And to figure out the puzzle of Esmerelda Clark.

His mind turned back to that last moment before she'd fled the cottage. The snap of electricity between them, the tantalizing spread of color from the V-neck of her shirt up her neck, the wariness mixed with desire in her vivid green eyes…he'd been ensnared. Intoxicated.

And she'd run.

The desire to pursue, to catch and demand answers,

had been strong. But from what little he'd learned of Esmerelda, patience would serve him better. Her flight, coupled with the sensual tension between them, had confirmed that there had been something more to their relationship than simple professionalism.

The next few weeks would give him the chance to heal, but also the opportunity to break down whatever barriers he'd erected between him and Esme in his previous life and uncover the truth.

What if she's telling the truth? That you were simply a cold, callous bastard?

Was he pursuing Esmerelda because she was the one thing he could remember? Had he created the memory of them, naked and wrapped around each other in a lovers' embrace,i because he had needed something, anything, to grasp onto? Or had an unrequited attraction surfaced from his trauma? Had it been one-sided on his part?

Uncomfortable thoughts. Yet none of them felt right. And whether they had been lovers or not, something terrible had happened between him and Esmerelda. Something that had severed his relationship with the woman who been his sworn protector.

His mind opened unexpectedly—just for a moment—but it was long enough. He saw Esmerelda's face, her freckles standing out starkly against pale skin as she stared at him, eyes shining bright with unshed tears. A memory, and a vivid one. Pain hit him in the chest, hard and ugly, along with a remembered determination that pushed him on to do what he had to do...

A wall rose up. He inwardly swore as the headache turned sharp, combining pressure with tiny hot pricks like a dagger held over an open flame being driven into his skull again and again. Were all his first memories going to be so painful?

Several minutes passed before the headache lessened enough for him to focus on other things. He glanced at his watch. It had been nearly an hour since Esmerelda had left. An hour that he had put to good use. But he didn't like how long she'd been gone. Yes, the woman could obviously take care of herself. But each passing moment was another moment she could be using to get away from Grenada, to disappear once again.

His chest tightened. Then loosened as he heard the creak of footsteps on the stairs. Esmerelda appeared at the top a moment later, her hair pulled into a loose bun on top of her head, errant curls slipping down to frame her face. A cloth bag hung over one shoulder.

"Groceries," she said as she caught his curious glance at the bag. "Not much, but enough to get us through today and tomorrow."

"Thank you."

She nodded, then moved quickly past him into the cottage. He waited a moment, assembled his thoughts, reviewed his strategy, then followed her inside.

"I got in touch with Burak. He wasn't happy about my supposed change in itinerary, but he's made arrangements for me."

"Good."

He watched as she pulled out a knife and cutting board and started chopping up fruit.

"One of the arrangements is a residence here on the island. Larger than this one."

Much larger.

The knife blade slowed in its downward arc and became stuck in the papaya Esme had been slicing.

"You're leaving then?"

"I am."

She looked up, blinked rapidly, then nodded as her breath whooshed out.

"Good. That's good."

"I'd like you to come with me."

A frown appeared.

"I'm not going back to Rodina."

"Neither am I. Not for at least two weeks. I'm staying here on Grenada."

Her lips parted.

"You're what?"

"I'm staying. And I'd like for you to stay with me."

"Perhaps I didn't make it clear." She set the knife down carefully, as if she was trying to resist the temptation to stab him with it. "I want nothing more to do with you. I am sorry about your accident, but you expressed that you had no interest in working with me anymore."

"And now I'm saying otherwise."

"You can't just change your mind like that!" She went from simmering frustration to full-blown anger in seconds. "I've moved on. If you haven't noticed, I left the country I was born and raised in and decided to travel halfway around the world thinking that I might just have a slight amount of time to get myself together before tackling the next phase of my life, only to have the man who fired me from his team chase me halfway across the world and show up on my private beach that I paid good money for. Do you think you can just waltz in here and take over my life once more? Do you truly think that after you…"

She paused then, as if trying to get her words right before she spoke. He made note of it, filed it away for later.

"After you reassigned me without talking to me at all,

just dropped this bombshell on me with no warning, you assigned me to a role that I had expressed that I was not interested in in the slightest, that I would just give in to your demands?"

"I did think that having amnesia might make a difference."

"Well, it doesn't," she fired back. "I'm getting on with my life. You should do the same."

"I'll ensure you have a reference for future employers. I will also pay you one hundred thousand euros for you to serve as my bodyguard."

Her eyebrows climbed up to her hairline.

"That's nearly a year's salary."

"I'm interrupting your vacation. And after firing you. Paying you an outrageous sum seems like the least I could do."

He smiled, a slow, sensual smile designed to tempt. And tempt it did. Not that it would make a difference."

Her eyes narrowed. "Is that all I'm expected to do? Or would there be other duties as assigned?"

"Such as?"

"Sharing your bed."

Fury ripped through him.

"That's not what I would be purchasing, Miss Clark."

She blinked at the chill in his voice, then surprised him as a chilly yet satisfied smile slowly tilted her lips up.

"You might have lost your memory, Your Highness, but you're still in there. Just as cold and bastardly as ever."

With that, she turned to leave. He went after her, his long strides eating up the distance between them. He caught her elbow and turned her around.

"Then I'll try a different tactic."

She yanked her arm away.

"There's nothing you can say that will make me—"

"Please."

She stared at him, stunned.

"What?"

"Please, Miss Clark. Maybe by the time I return to Rodina, my memory will have returned. But if it doesn't, then I will be stepping into a role that literally impacts people's lives. I will do far better if I have time to recover, and recover with the presence of someone who feels familiar to me. Someone who knows me, better than I know myself."

She was bending. He saw it in the way she bit down on her lips, crossed her arms over her chest as if to ward him off even as her defenses began to crumble.

"Why can't Burak fly over—?"

"I don't know him."

She frowned.

"You don't remember me either—"

"You're the only person in my life, or rather my former life, with whom I feel any recognition. With you, I feel calm. My recovery will go better if I were to have someone near that I'm comfortable with. It might even help speed up the process of me regaining my memory."

She stared at him, evaluating. Could she see that he had another agenda in mind? Yes, everything he was saying was true. But he also wanted to find out what had happened between them, to get to know the woman who stood before him. To understand the attraction that flared in her eyes every time she was near him. To understand why he was so sure that what had happened between them had been life-changing. To understand his reaction to Esme Clark, the way she made his blood heat.

Her breath came out in a rush, followed by a softly muttered curse.

"And what if you don't recover your memory?"

"No matter what does, or does not, happen, I will return to my role within the palace." He paused, watching her. "You told me the one thing you know for certain is that you love your country. If you love it so much, help me."

Her head snapped up.

"Don't you dare use that to manipulate me."

"I'm only trying to manipulate you a little." At her raised brow, he held up his hands. "Okay, I'm trying to manipulate quite a bit. But there's truth in what I have to say, too. You love your country. And right now, your country needs you. The family you once served needs you. That it will give me a chance to right the wrong I did to you is a bonus I probably don't deserve."

She stared at him for so long he wondered if she would say no.

And then she sighed. Triumph surged inside him.

"I don't like this."

"Don't like what?"

"I don't like the uncertainty, giving up the time I planned for myself." She tugged at the band holding up her hair, reddish gold curls tumbling down over her shoulders in a riotous cascade that made the seductive memory flare once more. "I lived for years with someone else making choices for me, arranging my life to suit their desires and wants. I'm not going back down that road again. Not just when I've broken free."

He regally inclined his head to her.

"I will not ask anything of you beyond these two weeks."

She arched a brow.

"Unless you change your mind and want something else," she said knowingly.

His eyes glinted again, but this time with humor.

"It depends on what I want and how badly I want it."

CHAPTER SEVEN

THE SUN ROSE over the eastern waters of the Caribbean Sea. Waves rose, turned golden by the sunlight, before splashing back down into blue-and-white foam. A seagull cawed in the distance. Manicured green lawns raced down to the private beach of fluffy white sand, the yard dotted here and there with a soaring palm tree or a well-tended bed of bright blooms.

Idyllic. Perfect. And Esme wasn't enjoying a single moment.

A yawn escaped her as she snuggled deeper into the robe she'd found in the bathroom. Luxurious and cozy, it warded off the early morning chill. Within an hour, she knew the temperatures would climb steadily and drive vacationers into the ocean waters or the nearest pool.

But for now, with a gentle breeze bringing just a touch of coolness off the water, it was soothing.

She needed soothing after the night she'd had. Once she'd said yes to the devil and agreed to accompany him for two weeks to his "new residence," she'd packed her tiny suitcase and walked with him down to the beach. A dinghy had been waiting and carried them out to an impressive two-story catamaran with big white sails that had ballooned out under the captain's expert skill and taken them south to Prickly Bay and the exclusive Lance aux Epines community.

It wasn't like she hadn't been exposed to wealth and luxury in her year on Julius's security team. But when her eyes were roving over crowds of people assessing for threats, when she was mentally evaluating potential exits in case of various hazards or disasters, she hadn't done much ogling.

Julius hadn't said much on the boat. In fact, he had been nothing but a gentleman since she had agreed to accompany him. All sensuality had disappeared, replaced by a man who was certainly friendlier and softer than Prince Julius Carvalho, but far removed from the man whose eyes had burned with desire as for one heart-pounding moment she thought he'd kiss her.

But he hadn't. Once she said yes, it was as if he pulled back whatever he felt, or thought he felt for her, and was striving to show her he could behave himself. Would not ask more of her than he already had. And wasn't that what she wanted? That she found herself missing the tension, the spark of desire, had only made her cranky and short with him. A pity, because the sail down the coast to Prickly Bay had been peaceful, the crew professional, and the views unparalleled.

And when the boat had pulled up to the private dock of the Dove Villa, it had been almost like a fairy tale. Cinderella's coach, or in this case sailboat, pulling up to the palace.

The villa was beautiful. No, not just beautiful. Stunning. An architectural wonder. Gleaming ivory walls offset by white pillars guarded the two-story front door. Yet instead of appearing so expensive she was afraid to step inside, the red tiled roof had added a touch of relaxation to the otherwise austere exterior. Inside met outside with the sliding walls of glass that could be rolled into recesses in the wall and open the massive rooms to blue sky and ocean breezes.

Julius had reached out a hand to help her off the catamaran onto the dock. She'd walked off herself, regretting the petulant move when he'd simply turned away and walked up the path to the villa. A butler, Aroldo, had met them and given them a tour.

The furniture was understated, a mix of whites and blues, yet of obviously high quality. More white pillars held up soaring ceilings and made room for large fans that rotated silently as they kept the villa pleasantly cool during the hot afternoons. Tiles faded to a soft red dominated the main rooms, while weathered gray hardwood added both elegance and relaxation to the bedrooms.

Julius had thanked Aroldo and asked him to show Esme to her room before bowing his head to her.

"Perhaps I'll see you at dinner."

But she hadn't. She hadn't seen him all evening. Restless, she'd unpacked, then re-sorted how she'd hung up her meager clothes. She'd prowled online job listings, waiting for something to click, to feel right.

Waiting for a knock at the door. She'd waited in vain.

She'd tried to focus on the beauty of her room. A large bed stood in the center, thick white pillows arranged perfectly against a light gray headboard. Opposite the bed sat a couch, this one covered in the same gray material as the headboard, with a large window just above the back that overlooked the expansive grounds. To her left lay the bathroom, with a freestanding white marble tub in front of a wall covered in mosaic tiles of emerald and scarlet red arranged into a tropical flower against a brilliant blue sky. To her right, the entire wall was comprised of glass, including two massive doors that opened onto a private terrace with steps descending to the infinity pool.

The rooms balanced elegance with relaxation, quality with comfort. Yet the location and the investments in furnishings, from the lamp stands fashioned of gold to the crystal vase overflowing with red roses, made it clearly known that this was the kind of place only the wealthiest could afford.

But even the loveliness of her surroundings could only soothe for so long. Growing edginess had driven her into the kitchen shortly after sundown. A bowl of *pelau* had been left for her in the fridge with heating instructions, along with a note from Aroldo inviting her to help herself to anything in the kitchen and to call if she needed something. The chicken and rice dish, made heartier with a mix of carrots, celery, beans, red peppers and a dash of brown sugar, had assuaged her physical hunger.

Yet still she felt hollow. Empty.

It wasn't just Julius, although he certainly played a significant role. She had questioned her decision to follow him so quickly, how a simple "please" had led to her changing her mind, and her plans, for the next two weeks. All for a man who had broken her heart.

Part of it, she was coming to realize, was because in some twisted way, Julius had tossed her a lifeline. Two more weeks of something else to focus on other than what she was going to do with the rest of her life. How she was going to shape it just the way she wanted, without outside pressure. Without bending to the whims of someone else.

"Good morning."

Her lips firmed into a frown even as her heartbeat

quickened at the sound of his voice. The second time in less than twenty-four hours the man had snuck up on her.

"Good morning, Your Highness."

Tension rolled off him as he sat in the lounge chair next to hers.

"Please call me Julius."

"Saying 'please' isn't going to get you everything you want." She glanced at him then, her chest tightening as the sun added golden highlights to his dark blond hair. "I spent a year referring to you as 'Your Highness,' 'sir,' et cetera. Hard to break that habit."

"It's odd," he mused, staring out over the ocean, "but when you use those titles, it makes me feel...distant. Almost tired."

Surprised, she glanced at him fully. He wore a white shirt unbuttoned at the collar with the sleeves rolled up, dark blue pants and... She blinked. Barefoot. The Crown Prince of Rodina was barefoot. Julius almost never went anywhere without a tie. He certainly never went barefoot.

Except for Paris.

She pushed the thought away.

"You carried a great deal on your shoulders."

"Did I?"

"Yes. You sit on multiple committees, including finance and transportation. You were also involved in military operations and, your personal cause, education."

"Given how little you seem to think of me as a man, I'm surprised by the respect in your voice."

She shrugged.

"Great leaders can be very different behind closed doors."

Silence followed. She forced herself to lean back in her

chair, to focus on the crystal-clear waters of the pool, the ocean just beyond.

"Tell me why my reassignment of you hurt so much. Please," he added with the hint of a smile as she arched one brow.

The obvious answer, that she had fallen in love with and slept with her boss, wouldn't do. Yet as she turned his question over in her mind, she analyzed it in a way she hadn't before.

"I was embarrassed." Truth added a rawness to her voice that made her clear her throat. "My father is the head of palace security. He lives for his work. Always has. I had considered going to the States for graduate studies after I got my degree. Something around law or political science. He suggested I go through the academy." Over two decades of pain rose up and wrapped around her heart like a vise. "It was the first time he had shown interest in what I did. So I did what he suggested. I was out in six months, completed another three months of advanced training at the commandant's recommendation. Assigned to general palace security for six months when I graduated, and then your detail the following year."

"Your father must have been proud."

She shrugged to mask the hurt. "As much as he was capable of being. Still, I grasped onto the crumbs of his approval like it was a lifeline. And..." She could feel the blush rising up her throat, that damned telltale hotness that made her feel transparent, vulnerable. "Others were more impressed. Each compliment, each commendation, made me feel whole for the first time in my life. When I was promoted to your detail a few months before my twenty-fifth birthday, for the first time in my life my father said 'well done.'"

"I took that away from you."

A warm hand settled on top of hers. Startled, she turned to look at him. She'd glimpsed occasional flickers of kindness in Julius. But the understanding on this man's face, so familiar yet so different, from the compassion in his gaze to the regret that pulled at the corners of his mouth, touched her in a way she wasn't ready for.

"Yes." She pulled her hand back. Did she imagine the hurt that flashed in his eyes before he settled back in his chair? "That's what it felt like. I didn't have any warning."

"I'm sorry."

She gave him a small, sad smile. "How can you be sorry for something you don't even remember?"

He looked out over the ocean, a small frown forming between his brows.

"I do remember it. Some of it at least."

Panic skittered down her spine.

"Oh?"

"Your face. You looked heartbroken." He looked back at her then. "And I put that there. That pain in your eyes. After you swore to protect me with your life."

Guilt settled on her shoulders, heavy and clawing. She didn't want to tell him, didn't know if it was the right thing to tell him so soon after the onset of his amnesia.

"I was angry. And hurt. But it was within your right to reassign me."

"Not if it made you hurt, Esmerelda."

The way her name rolled off his tongue made a shiver pass over her skin. Not ready to confront the desire that still lingered in her veins.

"I appreciate the apology, sir. I will get over it."

"I suspect you're a woman who rises to the occasion or surpasses it more often than not. But tell me," he said, leaning forward, filling up her vision and her senses with his closeness, "how often do you make that journey alone?"

His voice filled her, winding through her and warming her blood.

Her phone dinged. Grateful for the reprieve from diving any deeper into her past, she pulled it out of the pocket of her robe. She muttered a curse as she read the text.

"Something wrong?"

"I emailed a friend at Scotland Yard to ask about any reports of muggings or assaults near the hotel you were staying at." She sighed. "Nothing."

"The doctor said it looked like a blow from a blunt object."

She frowned. "When did you see a doctor?"

"A doctor from one of the resorts in St. George's came by last night." Julius's fingers wandered to the back of his neck, crept up to rest lightly on the wound. "No evidence of any lingering concussion, although I do have an appointment this afternoon for some scans."

"And the memory loss?"

Julius's lips thinned. "Hopefully temporary. The head wound is unfortunate, but other than the loss of consciousness and initial nausea when I woke up, there's no evidence I'm still suffering from a concussion."

Confused, Esme propped her chin on her hand.

"So what does that mean?"

"Most likely dissociative retrograde amnesia."

"Pardon?"

"It means I saw something scary and disassociated from the event by forgetting everything about my previous life."

The words came out as a growl. Esme felt herself slip back into her old role, the one of peacemaker, of guard and protector.

"You're angry at yourself."

"Extremely."

"Because you feel weak."

"Aren't I?" he snapped. "Apparently I saw something frightening and instead of facing it, I retreated into my worthless mind."

"Your mind's not worthless, Julius."

Her use of his first name did what it was intended. His shoulders relaxed, his frown lessening as he blew out a harsh breath.

"It is disconcerting to think I ran from danger. Even more so when I hear how I treated my employees." His laugh was short and humorless. "I shudder to think of the ruler I was. What kind of ruler I will become."

The guilt gnawed deeper, making her sick.

"Julius—"

"No more." He suddenly looked tired, the shadows beneath his eyes darker and more pronounced. "I am in need of a walk."

He stood and moved to the edge of the terrace. She pulled the lapels of her robe closer, seeking comfort in the plush material. She needed to talk to the doctor who had treated him, find out if telling him the truth would be better or worse for his recovery. Because keeping the secret of their time together was feeling more and more selfish. Yes, he'd hurt her. But he also hadn't outright fired her. He had also made it clear in Paris that what they would have would be temporary.

She'd been the one to go and fall in love. To think they might have more than just one night. She knew he would have to marry someone suitable. The he was meant for someone else.

"Esmerelda?"

She blinked and focused on him.

"Sorry. What did you say?"

"Would you like to join me?"

"Oh. I don't want to interrupt—"

"I would prefer the company of someone else than just my own," he said with a sardonic smile.

"Of course, sir."

"Julius."

He said it softly, but the single word was threaded with steel. She hesitated. It would be a submission. Surrender.

Part of her argued it was the best thing she could do given everything he'd been through. The still aching part of her soul fired back that after he'd cut her loose in such a cold manner, had taken away the career she had told him had been so important to her, he didn't deserve any capitulation.

But when she silenced those voices, focused on her heart, she found that the answer was simple.

"Thank you… Julius."

Triumph flashed in his whiskey-brown eyes. Suddenly afraid that she had given up something valuable, she fumbled for an excuse to go inside, to flee to the safety of her luxurious room.

Warm fingers curled around hers. Her heart stopped, then slammed into overdrive. Her feet moved of their own accord, following Julius as he gently but firmly pulled her down the deck to the stairs.

Minutes later, they arrived at the beach, hands still entwined. Every time she started to pull away, his fingers tightened just enough that to pull away would have been obvious.

Worst of all, she didn't want to. Even during their all-too-brief romantic interlude, they had never held hands. It made her feel young, cherished, protected.

"Oh!"

The exclamation escaped her lips before she could stop it. Up ahead, hanging from the tops of two massive palm trees, was a wooden swing.

"Do you like to swing?"

"I'm not sure."

She felt Julius's gaze on her, felt it burn through her.

"How can you not be sure? I have amnesia, and even I feel comforted by the sight of a swing."

"I never had a playset growing up," she admitted. "Beautiful toys, things to keep myself company. But nothing like a swing or a slide. My mother didn't like getting her hands dirty and preferred the label on the toy versus the functionality. My father worked too much to be concerned with trivial matters."

"Trivial matters?" Julius repeated. Disdain dripped from his voice. "How is raising a child trivial?"

"I was not intended. My mother and father were dating. I came along. They never even married. They lived together for years, although my mother made frequent long trips back to Scotland and England. My father just wasn't interested in children. My mother preferred a more exciting life. Having a small child hindered that."

It hurt less to talk about now. She had never once been wanted. Not until her surprisingly successful career in security. Not until she had, for one brief moment, been wanted by a man without condition, simply because he desired her. And it had been because of that she had had the courage to walk away from everything. Because of the knowledge that it was possible, even if that man's dismissal of her had been the most painful thing she'd ever had to go through.

"Where is your mother now?"

"America. She met a doctor when I was thirteen, had a whirlwind courtship and now spends her days lunching and sunning by a pool."

"And your father didn't care?"

"I believe he shrugged and said he hoped she was happy. He doesn't care about much other than his job."

A long pause ensued, broken up only by the surf cascading onto the white sandy beach.

"I'm not certain of many things these days," Julius finally said, "but I'm certain I would not like your parents."

She stifled the retort that came automatically to mind. For too long she had defended her parents and their lackadaisical attempts at serving in the roles of mother and father. Had wanted to believe that they cared more than they did.

"I don't much like them myself. I love them," she added thoughtfully, "as I imagine many children love the caretakers they know. They don't know anything else, or any better."

Another beat of silence ensued.

"What is my relationship like? With my father?"

His voice sounded strong, steady. Yet underneath she heard the current of uncertainty, the slight twist of doubt.

"On the outside, amiable. Mutual respect, partnering on various political and legal matters." She turned to face him then, wanting him to see the truth. "In private, he loves you very much, as you do him. The pressure you've placed on yourself to succeed comes primarily from within." She hesitated. "I'm not sure from where. We didn't have the kind of relationship where you would have shared what drove you. But your father believes in you. He knows you will be a good leader."

Julius regarded her for a long moment before taking her other hand in his and squeezing them both.

"Obrigado." He cast a glance at the swing, then back at her. "You should get on."

She chuckled. "I don't think many twenty-six-year-olds swing."

He stepped closer, both hands still wrapped around hers. Her breath caught in her chest as she tilted her chin up to look at him.

"You wanted to figure out what you wanted from your life." He nodded toward the swing. "Seems like a simple step. Does Esmerelda Clark like to swing or not? Find out."

When he phrased it like that, it did seem extraordinarily simple. She stepped back, missing the touch of his hands even as she hated that she missed it. She turned away and slipped onto the swing. The wood was warm from the sun. The ropes were made of thick twine, scratchy against her palms. She dug her toes into the sand and prepared to push off.

The swing gave a tug. Startled, she looked up to see Julius's hands wrapped around the ropes.

"Hold on."

His words whispered over her. He pulled back, then let go. A moment later she flew out over the water, blue beneath her and above. Startled by the sensation of flying, of weightlessness as she reached the pinnacle, she threw back her head and laughed.

She didn't how long Julius pushed her on the swing. Probably only a minute or two, but it felt like one of those blissful moments in time that stretched forever, where the rest of the world faded away and left nothing but contented pleasure.

She glanced back over her shoulder with a grin. And nearly fell off as Julius suddenly stopped the swing.

"What—"

He circled around, his hands still on the ropes, caging her between his body and the swing. The morning heat changed, crackling with sensual tension as she looked up at him. The whiskey brown had turned almost golden as he gazed down at her.

"You've smiled at me like that before."

Her throat constricted.

"What?"

"You smiled at me like that before," he repeated. His eyes took on a faraway look as his mind tried to grasp the past. "In… Paris. We were in Paris. There was a café and flowers. I said something to you, and you laughed and smiled at me."

"Okay."

She tried to stand up, but he held his ground. She sat back down, unwilling to put her body against his, not with this electricity humming between them.

"I don't know if you realize this, but people do smile and laugh at each other. Even princes and their bodyguards."

"This was different," he insisted. He leaned down until she could see the dark flecks in his eyes, could smell the rich scent of cedar rolling off his skin. "I saw it in your eyes. You felt something for me. Tell me what it was, Esme."

Her fingers tightened around the ropes. She couldn't lie. She had already stretched and twisted the truth enough, justified her insistence that they were not lovers. But what could she say now? This Julius, the softer, protective, yet no less commanding man who had emerged from whatever atrocity had occurred in London, could entice her back into his arms. Into his bed. He would insist the few idealistic memories he had of her meant they were to be together. And damn it, with how raw her still hurting heart was, she didn't know if she would have the strength to resist.

Only for him to go back to Rodina and assume his responsibilities. To marry another woman, to have children with her.

Or worse…for him to remember. To remember and look at her once more like she was nothing more than a woman he had had one night with and no more.

"I don't think your memories can be considered reliable given what's happened, sir."

The words had their intended effect, as did her formal address. He released the ropes and stepped back. She surged to her feet and hurried up the beach toward the path, not caring if she looked guilty or not.

"Esmerelda."

Oh, how she wanted to keep running. But wasn't that what she had been doing for over a month? Running away, running toward something, even if she didn't know what that something was?

She forced herself to stop, to turn and face him. He stood on the beach, shoulders thrown back, the wind ruffling his hair. Even from this distance, she could see the regality on his chiseled features, feel his confusion and anger.

"I will find out the truth," he shouted, his face hard and unyielding. "That's a promise."

CHAPTER EIGHT

JULIUS AWOKE WITH the memory of funeral music pulsing through his veins, as if he'd been hollowed out by grief. The image of a woman with hair as blond as his, her kind face covered in makeup to make her look in death as she had in life, was seared into his brain.

Throwing back the covers, he stood and strode to the glass doors overlooking the ocean. His chest rose and fell as he tried to get a handle on his racing heart, his erratic breathing. Hard to do when the grief he'd felt at his mother's funeral over twenty years ago flooded him as fresh as if he'd watched her coffin lowered into the ground yesterday.

He pressed his forehead to the glass. The coolness soothed the hot sweat on his brow, grounded him in the moment.

Elizabeth.

Her name came to him, a whisper in his mind that pulled up memories of warm hugs, a soothing voice tinged with a British accent, and the scent of violets. Each remembrance, of a kiss to his forehead after falling into the cold waves at some nameless beach, of sitting on a couch under a blanket watching some black-and-white movie, was both a godsend and a stab to his heart.

Gradually, the memories receded, leaving behind a different type of emptiness. He had wanted this, had craved a connection to his past. But remembering his mother, the things he had loved about her, made the knowledge that she was gone and had been gone for years even more painful. Like having a cherished treasure dangled before one's eyes only to have it yanked away moments later.

One deep breath, then another. Slowly, he accepted his grief, the newfound memories. Perhaps tomorrow, or the day after, he would revisit them, honor his mother as best he could.

But now, with the wound of loss so fresh, he needed to pause. The reopening of his grief had brought with it a faint memory of why he had withdrawn from the world, become the cold, hard man he'd witnessed in the photographs, heard about from Esme's account of his reassigning her. It wasn't a complete picture, more like a puzzle with important pieces still missing. But he had the gist of what had happened.

He'd been hurt. As people tend to do when they're in pain, he'd withdrawn. Unlike others, who had healed and gradually rejoined the world, he was beginning to suspect he'd burrowed himself deep into a hole of apathy.

A suspicion that made loathing churn in his stomach. If the doctor was right, he'd run from something in London. Even though he knew there was more to his and Esme's story than what she was sharing, he didn't doubt her grief, her humiliation, when she told him about his firing her from his detail. He wanted to remember. But, he wondered as he pulled the glass doors apart and stepped out onto the terrace, did he truly?

A sigh escaped him as he moved to the railing. Was this to be his life for the foreseeable future? Wanting his memories to return, yet being on guard as to when they would appear and how emotional they would be?

Remembering Esmerelda's face when he'd delivered the news of her reassignment had been a punch to the gut. Yet seeing her smile so vividly, the emotion in her eyes, had warmed him.

Until she had sworn that he had misinterpreted the memory, just as he had his first recollection of her.

He didn't believe her. Not about their personal history. It was an odd sensation, to entrust one's life to someone knowing they were concealing something. But despite her perfidy, he still felt as soothed by her presence as he did fired up by the passion swirling like a tornado between them, still experienced the thrill of a connection rooted somewhere in his murky past whenever she was near.

Although since their short sojourn onto the beach, he hadn't talked with her in over two days. When he'd gone to the hospital for his scans, she'd sat upfront with the driver, stayed quiet in a corner as machines had whirred about his head. Nothing of concern had been noted. The doctor had reiterated his initial instructions.

"Rest. Relax. I'm confident your memories will come back."

They'd returned to the villa and Esmerelda had promptly disappeared. The evening staff had drifted in just after five and prepared dinner. The butler, Aroldo, had mentioned that Esmerelda had dined in her room, then gone out for a walk around the grounds. The same had happened yesterday. He'd spotted her here and there, eyes scanning the landscape, occasionally walking the perimeter of the grounds when he ventured outside.

Doing her job, yes. But she didn't have to ignore him.

Her evasion grated, as did how much it bothered him.

He would not allow her to do the same tonight. Tonight he would take the tray himself if necessary—

"Good morning."

Soft, delicate, with a tinge of huskiness that brushed over his skin. Esme stood just outside the doors to her room, her curls pulled up into a ponytail, leaving her freckled face bare to his hungry gaze.

"Good morning."

She smiled, the gesture doing little to belie the wariness lurking in her eyes, as if she were afraid he might pounce.

"I was going…" Her voice trailed off. "Would you…?"

"Have you always been this eloquent?"

Red tinged her cheeks at his teasing tone. Whoever had told her that nonsense about flushing or whatever term it was had been a fool. The woman was a beautiful blend of colors: tan skin beneath coffee freckles, emerald-green eyes, red hair threaded with gold.

"I'm going to take one of the boats out." The faint pride in her voice had him suppressing a smile. "Would you like to join me?"

"Two days ago you could barely stand to be in my company." He cocked his head to one side. "Now you're proposing a boat ride?"

"I'm going out. You're welcome to join me or not."

She turned away and started for the stairs. His esteem rose, as did the intrigue surrounding this enigmatic woman. She had a backbone. He liked that about her.

"I'll be down in five."

She glanced over her shoulder, nodded once to shown she'd heard him and then continued on. He watched as she moved down the path until she disappeared around a corner. Whatever her motives were in inviting him out onto the ocean, it would give him time to get to know her better since she'd kept him at a distance the past forty-eight hours.

Four minutes later he strode onto the dock. A sleek, spacious speedboat greeted him. Portholes indicated a cabin belowdeck. Esme, seated at the helm, glanced up, her eyes hidden behind large sunglasses.

"Where are we headed?"

"The ocean."

"Did you always keep important details to yourself?" he asked as he climbed aboard and sank down onto a plush leather seat kept cool by an overhead canopy.

"Need to know, sir."

"Call me Julius."

"No thank you, sir." She tossed a saucy smile over her shoulder. "It's protocol, and I am your bodyguard."

"Yet you were something more."

Seated behind her, he couldn't miss the tensing of her shoulders beneath the white T-shirt, the tightening of her fingers around the steering wheel.

"Could we keep the past behind us? Just for an hour?"

She looked over her shoulder, her eyes hidden. But he could hear the vulnerability in her voice, the rawness that hinted at the depth of her pain. Pain that kept her from sharing the truth with him.

Suddenly angry with himself, regretting whatever he'd done to cause that pain, he nodded. She turned away and, gradually, her shoulders dropped, her body relaxing.

She guided them out of the bay with an easy confidence he admired. Even though a part of him wanted to grab the wheel, to take the helm and drive the boat across the waves, he knew he was in good hands.

An odd sensation, he reflected, as his gaze drifted over a sailboat cruising by. He felt that he was not the kind of man who handed over control easily. Based on what little he had remembered thus far, coupled with the minute details he'd gleaned from Esmerelda, Burak and the media, he seemed regimented, regulated almost to an extreme.

Was his ability to trust now, to place himself in the hands of someone he barely remembered, because he had no history to stop him from doing so? Or was it because of the woman at the wheel taking them further out onto the open ocean? This strong woman who had never been pushed on a swing and whose shocked laughter had stirred not just his desire but his heart?

Probably, he mused as he slid on his own pair of sunglasses as the sun glinted off the waves, a mixture of the two.

He shoved away his thoughts, leaned back into the seat and enjoyed the ride.

What was I thinking?

Esme glanced at a small mirror positioned on the dashboard that provided some protection from the ocean spray. Julius sat on the seat, arms draped casually along the back, his long legs stretched out. Wind ruffled his dark blond hair. Sunglasses now obscured his eyes so she couldn't tell if he was sleeping or watching the passing sea. In black swimming trunks and a gray T-shirt, he looked like any other beachgoer in the Caribbean.

Not at all like the disciplined prince she'd protected for over a year.

Over the past hour they'd barely exchanged five words. He'd appeared content to lay back and rest. That he trusted her and didn't pester her with questions had unnerved her as much as it had touched her. Julius had placed his trust in her before in a professional capacity. But then he'd had an entire dossier on her, not to mention security clearances, reviews of the very small number of men she'd dated and several extensive interviews that had felt more like inquisitions.

Now, he had a handful of memories and thirty-five years of emptiness. Yet still he trusted her.

Even though you're lying to him.

She pushed that uncomfortable thought away. Not only was she evading his questions, all created by her initial distortion of the truth, but she had lied to him this morning, too. She'd awoken just after sunrise and gone out onto the deck. It had been impossible to miss the sounds of someone clutched in the throes of a nightmare coming from the open window to his room. She'd had to force herself not to go to him, especially when she'd heard him gasp a word that had brought tears to her eyes.

"Mãe."

He'd been dreaming of his mother. He'd only been fourteen when Her Majesty the Queen had passed away. Esme had been five. All she could remember of the event was dressing in black and standing next to her mother as vehicle after vehicle had passed by in a funeral procession, the people around her weeping and tossing flowers onto the street. The first four months she'd been a part of his detail, he hadn't said a word about his mother. But after the parade incident and her ending up in the hospital, he'd mentioned her occasionally. Little things, like commenting that his mother would have found an ambassador at a dinner in Lisbon amusing or that she would have liked a painting at the Louvre. She had thought those confidences an indicator that they had grown closer after the accident.

Reading too much into something simple, she told herself. *Desperate for anything anyone would give you.*

The past was the past. She'd made choices she had to live with. For now, she had followed the instinct of inviting Julius out onto the water and distracting him from whatever nightmare he'd lived through last night.

"Am I seeing things?"

She grinned.

"What do you see?"

"An umbrella sticking up out of the middle of the ocean."

"Welcome to Mopion."

The tiny speck of land rose out of the water, white sand topped with a wood-and-thatch umbrella. Esme anchored the boat just off the reef. After a short ride in the dinghy that skimmed over colorful coral and fish, Julius hopped out and hauled the boat onto the sand.

"Beautiful." He glanced around with a slight smile. "Although after walking the length of it in less than thirty seconds, I'm not sure what else there is to do."

"Swim. Snorkel. Relax. There's a cooler for when we get back on the boat, too."

She smoothed her hands over the white swim shirt she wore as protection against the blazing sun. It provided some security. But her decision to wear bikini bottoms was now inspiring doubt. She felt naked, vulnerable, with so much skin on display.

"Take a look at this."

Julius wasn't ogling or even sneaking covert glances at her. No, he was examining the pole of the umbrella. Telling herself she was relieved instead of disappointed, she moved up the sand.

"Initials," she said with a small smile. "There's so many."

Some were simple letters, others with hearts, stars and even a few Cupid's arrows.

"Looks like a popular place." Julius looked around. "Although not today. There's hardly a boat in sight."

"Hurricane season."

"So naturally you came here."

She shrugged as she stood and moved back toward the water.

"Affordable, and Grenada is far enough south that it rarely gets hit. Plus," she said as she tossed a smile over her shoulder and stretched out her arms, doing a spin in the sand, "I get to enjoy places like this all to myself."

Julius moved suddenly, stopping her midtwirl by placing his hands on her waist. She grabbed onto his shoulders to steady herself. His touch made her suck in a breath before she could summon her defenses.

"Why did you invite me today?"

She hesitated. The old Julius would have been apathetic at best, and coldly furious at worst, to know someone had witnessed a moment of vulnerability. How would the new Julius handle it?

"I heard you this morning. Dreaming." She tilted her head to the side as she watched him: the surprise that flickered in his eyes, the thinning of his lips. "Or perhaps remembering."

Slowly, he released her. A chill raked over her skin despite the sun burning overhead as she took a step back.

"Remembering."

Surprised, she watched him as he walked a few feet away and stared out over the ocean.

"I remembered my mother. Elizabeth. I remembered her death. Her funeral. A couple moments from my childhood."

What more was there to say? She had heard the grief in that one uttered word this morning. It had been strange to hear the depth of emotion in the voice of a man who so often seemed intractable. The brief flutter of panic she felt at hearing that he was remembering disappeared almost as quickly as it had come, her concern overriding her fear.

"She was by all accounts an incredible queen. She volunteered a lot. Engaged with the people."

"That sounds…familiar. Like her." He blew out a harsh breath. "I want to remember more."

What could she say to that? What would it be like to have one's entire life, the people they cared about, erased in a matter of seconds?

"I'm sorry."

He shrugged, his back to her.

"The doctor said any returning memories were a good sign."

"A good sign for your long-term health, yes. Doesn't mean you have to like what you remember."

He let out a low laugh.

"No, I suppose it doesn't."

She gave in to instinct, went to him as she had once before. This time, however, instead of stiffening beneath her touch the way he had the morning after their night together in Paris, he leaned into her touch.

Her heart pounded against her ribs, almost painfully. Her defenses wavered.

Dangerous. Too dangerous, a voice frantically whispered in her head.

Accepting her touch, opening himself to her. It all led to dangerous places where emotion crept through the cracks and weakened her resolve to keep her heart intact.

"Let's swim."

He turned. Her hand fell away, only for his to come up and brush strands of hair from her face.

"Thank you, Esmerelda."

Before she could come up with a response, he dropped his hand and moved away.

Oh, yes. She was in trouble.

Time flew as they slipped into the crystal-clear water and swam in lazy circles around the island. Aroldo had thoughtfully packed snorkel masks and fins, allowing them to strike out over the coral and spot schools of fish along with the occasional stingray resting on the sandy bottom. She kept a watchful eye out for passing boats and tourists lurking with cameras. But none appeared, leaving them cocooned in a rare moment of solitude.

By the time they climbed back into the dinghy and struck out for the boat, nearly two hours had passed. She was exhausted, the kind of exhaustion that accompanied a bone-deep contentment. Seeing the same state of relaxation on Julius's face, the sadness no longer in his eyes, made it even better.

Not, she realized with a slight smile as she climbed back on the boat and did another quick scan of the ocean, because she felt like she had to or because it had been the right thing to do. No, she'd done it because she had wanted to.

She disappeared belowdeck and changed into a white sundress. As she climbed back up to the deck, she pressed a button Aroldo had showed her that dropped the back sides of the boat down into an enlarged terrace. Julius, still in his swim trunks and with his muscled chest on display, set the cooler down on a countertop just behind the cockpit.

"Did you pack this?" he asked as he opened the cooler and glanced inside.

"No, Aroldo did."

Julius's smile flashed, quick and uninhibited. It stole her breath.

"That makes more sense."

He laid out containers of ripe strawberries, glistening mango and thick slices of cheese, along with shrimp, crab and several sauces. Esme's eyebrows climbed as he pulled out a bottle of champagne.

"It's barely noon."

"And you're on vacation."

"I'm working. Technically," she added with a touch of sass as he frowned, "I shouldn't even be drinking at all."

He poured two glasses and handed one to her.

"Your boss sounds terrible."

She laughed and accepted the glass. The sweet flavor of peach hit her tongue as bubbles danced down her throat.

"The old prince would never have drunk champagne, let alone had a drink before five."

A hint of darkness raced across his face.

"All the more reason to do it."

CHAPTER NINE

THEY PILED FOOD on their plates and moved to the stern of the boat. Julius sat on one of the leather lounges while she stretched out on a towel, one leg dangling over the side.

"What do you like to do in your spare time?"

She paused in the middle of popping a piece of rosemary-and-ginger chocolate into her mouth.

"Do?"

"You're obviously adept at handling a boat. And swimming. Do you spend all your time on the water?"

The chocolate turned bitter in her mouth. She tried to cover up her unease by taking a long drink of champagne.

"A decent bit," she finally said. "That and reading. Although I didn't get much time to myself when I worked for the palace."

"For me."

He lounged on the leather seat, his sunglasses back on, his body relaxed. Yet she knew better, knew what lurked beneath the surface. Not a relaxed wealthy vacationer, but a predator, a lion waiting to pounce.

"Yes."

"I find it curious that the woman I just spent the past two hours with has completely disappeared." He leaned forward. "As soon as I ask about you, you become tense."

"I don't like talking about myself."

"Why not?"

Whether it was the champagne or the sun or just the sudden fatigue of presenting a face to the world, she opted for the truth.

"Because I don't know that much about myself."

She could feel his surprise.

"How so?"

"I've always done what was expected. What others wanted." She pushed a strawberry around her plate, the fruit leaving a red smear of juice in its wake. "When I was five, that was wearing clothes I didn't like to please my mother. When I was thirteen, it was crying alone in my room when my mother moved away because my father didn't like tears."

"And when you joined the academy?"

She looked up then, faced him head-on.

"I wanted my father to be proud of me. I wanted... something. Any kind of connection." Her whole body grew tight, confusion spiraling through as questions she'd asked herself over and over again the past few weeks rose to the surface. "I went after a career I doubt I would have pursued had it not been for a childish wish."

"I imagine many others do the same."

Disappointment sliced through her. He didn't understand. She got up and set her plate on the counter, pulled on her dress as she walked back to the terrace and dropped onto her towel. She turned her gaze to the ocean, to the islands covered in lush green and sweeping mountains that dotted the blue waves.

"I'm sure they do," she finally said. "I love Rodina. I told myself when I first registered that loving my country would make up for picking a career that was my father's dream and not mine."

"Was it?"

"I don't know." She pulled her legs to her chest, rested her chin on her knees. "Even though I was good at it, I was never sure if it was something I wanted for myself or just because I was finally..."

She grasped for a word, a phrase, something that would give voice to the tumultuous storm that had been raging inside her for years, only recently brought to the surface when the one thing she'd been good at, the one thing she'd been recognized for, had been taken away.

All because she'd dared to grasp the one thing she had wanted, truly wanted just for herself, in her whole life.

The boat rocked beneath her. Shyness and embarrassment overtook her. She kept her eyes trained resolutely on the horizon, refusing to look at him. She'd been humiliated enough already.

The heat from his body as he sat next to her seeped through the thin material of her dress.

"I finally felt seen," she whispered.

He wrapped an arm around her shoulders. She stiffened, then surrendered to temptation and let her head relax against him.

"When I played upon your sense of duty and loyalty back in the cottage, you agreed almost immediately."

"You always were good at using people's emotions."

She said it without malice, but could still feel his body tense.

"I sound like a bastard."

"You could be." A sigh escaped her as she leaned deeper into his warmth. Utterly shameless.

Just one minute. One more minute and then I'll move.

"Then why did you keep working for me?"

"Because there was more to you than that. I didn't always agree with your methods, but I never doubted your intentions. You fought for the people. For the country."

Oh, how that had mesmerized her. To see someone who others viewed as cold, intractable, and yet come to see how deeply they cared. Unlike her mother, a vapid creature with no interests other than herself, and her father, addicted to his role but not the people he served, Julius's convictions had ensnared her, deepened her commitment to her role, to her country, to *him*.

"Wasn't there an abbot or some other religious figure who said the road to hell was paved with good intentions?"

His voice rumbled against her cheek.

"You are a good ruler, Julius. You and your father made me proud to be Rodinian."

He froze. Then his arm tightened and pulled her closer, enveloping her in that intoxicating cedar against the backdrop of sea air.

"How did I ever deserve you as my protector, Esmerelda?"

She lifted her head, turned to look at him. Her breath caught in her chest as she realized just how close their lips were. Her eyes moved from his mouth to his gaze. Need burned hot, making deep brown flare into amber. One hand came up, fingers grazing her jaw before they tangled in her hair and pulled her closer, stopping just shy of her mouth.

His lips parted. A whimper escaped, almost pleading, as need built in her, coiling her body tighter and tighter until she could barely resist it.

But she wouldn't be the first to yield. Not this time.

He murmured her name once more.

And then he kissed her.

Oh, dear heaven.

No slow, teasing kiss that had brought their bodies together in the Paris suite. This kiss claimed, conquered, branded. His lips moved over hers, confident and yet with a frantic edge that made her heart beat out of control as fire suffused her body.

He crushed her against his body. Delirious desire shot through her veins. She straddled his lap, her fingers sliding into his hair as she returned his kiss, pouring over a month's worth of longing and heartache into their embrace.

His tongue teased the seam of her mouth. Her lips parted and he plundered. With each stroke, energy pulsed through her. One hand stayed on her back and kept her anchored against him. The other quested upward, fingertips leaving a searing trail as they delved into her curls and pulled her head back. She arched against him, a protesting whimper escaping as he moved his mouth from hers. The whimper turned into a moan of satisfaction as he kissed the line of her jaw, down her neck, then lower still until his lips grazed the swells of her breasts.

"Julius…"

His hand moved from her back to her shoulder to the ties of her dress straps. She felt the material give as he pulled—

This is wrong.

The thought slammed into her. She wanted him. Dear God, how she wanted him. But they couldn't do this, couldn't make love, with so much unknown between them. With her lies hanging over them. And for all she knew Julius was engaged to another woman, or soon to be.

She started to say his name again, to tell him to wait while she gathered her thoughts. The sound of a boat horn cut across the water. Julius's head snapped up.

Relief mingled with disappointment as Esme scrambled to her feet and hastily tightened the straps on her dress.

"Looks like a yacht." She moved to the front where leather seats ringed the bow of the boat. "Still a half mile away. But they're heading in our direction. Just trying to give us a heads-up."

She waved in case anyone was watching through the binoculars, then turned.

Julius stood on the stern, his hands curled into fists at his sides. He stared at her with a hunger that made her feel like the most beautiful woman on earth even as it nearly frightened her with its intensity.

Had she wanted to be seen before? Because when he looked at her like this, as if he could see to the very depths of her soul and all the good and bad things inside her mind, it was both wonderful and terrifying.

"Esmerelda…"

She waited, apprehension chasing away the lingering traces of desire.

"I'm sorry."

Of all the things she had expected to hear, an apology was at the bottom of the list.

"Excuse me?"

"What happened here was wrong."

Bile rose in her throat, thick and bitter. She'd thought the same thing, but hearing it come out of Julius's mouth made her sick to her stomach. He didn't want her. He'd taken one taste and wanted no more. Nothing had changed. Nothing ever changed.

No. She was stronger. She was no longer depending on others for her own salvation. She wouldn't run, wouldn't crumble.

Her chin rose.

"I agree, sir."

He swore and started forward.

"That's not what I meant."

"It never is."

She moved, keeping one of the leather lounges between them. He stopped, his eyes narrowed to dangerous slits.

"Damn it, Esmerelda, listen to me—"

"That yacht is approaching quickly." She slipped back into her professional role, her voice void of emotion. "They may or may not have binoculars. They most certainly have phones or other recording devices onboard. If we want to ensure your anonymity, we need to go now."

Within a minute they were back on the water. She urged the boat's speed up as fast as she dared, wanting to get back to the villa, to put as much distance between herself and the island where she'd nearly made the second biggest mistake of her life.

Despite the wind rushing by, her focus shifting between the water and the navigation system, she knew the moment he moved to the seat behind hers.

"You misunderstood me."

"I didn't."

A string of colorful Portuguese curses sounded behind her.

"That's certainly new," she said, raising her voice to be heard over the wind. "I don't recall hearing you swear like a sailor."

"One has a right to swear when someone is refusing to listen."

A quick glance confirmed there were no boats anywhere nearby. She killed the engine, waiting until the boat slowed and began to drift with the current, keeping her gaze forward.

"I told you before when you first came to me that I was done listening to you." To her horror, tears pricked the backs of her eyes. "I gave in once. I'm not doing so again."

"I meant that nearly making love to you on the back of a boat in the middle of the Caribbean was wrong." She felt him just behind her, felt his tension and energy rippling off his body. "That giving in to our physical attraction was wrong when we haven't sorted out everything that happened between us before my accident."

The explanation made sense. Indeed, as her embarrassment cooled, it all sounded terribly rational. Which made her response seem all the more outlandish.

All the more dangerous. She'd submitted again, had allowed herself to be carried away by emotion. But all she was doing was digging her grave deeper. And what about Julius? If she did give in, what would happen when he did remember? Would this softer side of him disappear? Or would he keep aspects of the man she saw now, a man who loathed the thought of being married off to a woman he hadn't chosen for himself? A man who could potentially be hurt by an affair, too?

Suddenly overwhelmed by everything that had happened the past few days—Julius's unexpected arrival, his amnesia, their kiss—all hit at once and stripped away what few tatters remained of her pride.

"It's better to keep things unknown."

"Better for who, Esmerelda?"

She heard the accusation in his voice, the censure. She brushed it all aside as she grabbed the key still in the ignition.

"For both of us, Your Highness."

CHAPTER TEN

THE THIN THREAD of navy that clung to the horizon spread slowly upward, drenching the Caribbean Sea in darkness as day turned to night. Soft shades of pink and lavender decorated the sky above the villa. It reminded Julius of a painting he'd once seen at a museum in London, a decorated warship being pulled out to sea to be scrapped. A beautiful sunset that had deepened the sensation of loss, the passing of an era as an elegant ship past its prime was sent to a shipyard to be broken into pieces.

Another impression, a flash in time, of him standing before the painting, the gallery around him quiet as he'd stared, trying to reconcile his commitment to duty with an ache that hollowed out his chest and left him painfully empty.

A feeling he'd experienced once more when he'd heard the raw grief in Esmerelda's voice. When she had severed the connection between them. A connection that went beyond mere desire. A connection he had felt ever since he'd woken up to this new life.

Stars winked into existence overhead. They'd arrived back around one. Esmerelda had tied off the boat and walked back to the villa without a single glance in his direction. He'd debated following her, demanding answers, kissing her senseless and feeling her come alive beneath his touch again.

But he'd kept his distance, doing his damnedest to respect the boundaries she'd erected.

For now.

Had she simply been running from him again, he would have pursued. He was done with the subterfuge, the deception, what he suspected at this point were outright lies.

Yet he had kissed her as if his life had depended on it, had nearly stripped her bare and driven himself into her on the back of a boat where anyone could have seen them. That he had so nearly lost complete and total control had been unnerving to say the least. It had also struck at something deep inside, something innate that had risen from the dark and pulled him back.

His head dropped back against the back of his chair. It was odd to look at a vase and know that it was most likely a Waterford. To thank Aroldo in French without even thinking about translation when he'd come back to the villa. There were parts of himself that came naturally, logical aspects that were so ingrained not even a traumatic injury could wrench them away.

Yet what he suspected was one of the most critical moments of his life, a defining event involving a woman who had tried to help him today out of simple kindness, evaded him.

"...better to keep things unknown..."

Something pulled at his memory, a loose thread that dangled just out of reach. The more he tried to grasp it, to form an image of what had happened, the more his head started to pound.

He let out a growl as he exploded out of his chair. It was time for answers.

His suite included an alcove with bay windows that overlooked the bay and the faintest glimpse of the lighthouse. A pale gray desk with a slate-colored top stood in front of the windows, a laptop in the center.

So far, his searches had been restricted to himself, reading articles about suspected romances, goodwill trips to other countries and even archived stories dating back all the way to his birth. He'd also read up on his parents and Rodina.

The one person he hadn't searched had been Esmerelda. He'd wanted answers about her past, about who she was and who she had been to him, to come from her.

But that wasn't to be.

He typed in her name and "security guard Rodina." The first result, a video link, made him frown: *Bodyguard saves island prince from runaway horse.*

His chest tightened with dread. He clicked. It was from a little over a year ago, a parade through Rodina's capital. The video panned over floats from local schools, companies, the military. His father rode by in a sleek car, commentary from the video host noting the vehicle had been manufactured in one of Rodina's factories.

Then he saw himself, an odd sensation to watch as he walked behind the car, occasionally waving to the crowd with only the hint of a smile on his face. A stark contrast to the elegant yet friendlier waves of his father.

Esmerelda and a man he now recognized as Burak had walked just behind him. Both wore black suits with white shirts. Esmerelda's eyes roved, taking everything in, assessing. In the few seconds he watched her, he saw immediately why she had been so good at her job. She never stopped looking, alert as she soaked in details. He once again cursed her parents for eroding all sense of personal confidence.

Off-camera, someone shrieked. His heartbeat accelerated. Esmerelda's head whipped around. She didn't waste a second as she turned and ran toward Julius. A horse bounded onto screen, its rider frantically clinging to the reins even as he started to slide off.

Esmerelda was safe. Julius knew she was, had seen her with his own eyes just hours ago. That didn't stop his heart from pounding as he watched the horse rear up, watched Esmerelda push him out of the way just as the hooves came down on her back. She collapsed onto the road, rolling just as the horse reared up and came down again on her chest.

The camera zoomed in, capturing both Julius and Burak rushing to her side, before the feed cut off.

He slammed the lid of the computer shut and scrubbed his hands down his face.

It provided another piece of the puzzle, another clue as to what had happened between them. He couldn't remember, couldn't hear the sounds of the crowd, the scream of the horse, the shouts of terrified onlookers. But something told him his life had changed after that moment when Esmerelda had unflinchingly flung herself into harm's way to save his life.

Thinking about it now, he wanted nothing more than to storm her room and pull her into his arms. Touch her, reassure himself that she truly was all right.

To hell with it.

Esme jumped as a loud knock sounded on her door.

"Esmerelda. Open up."

Her eyes fluttered shut. She lay on her bed, curled up with a yellowed copy of her favorite Jane Austen novel.

The familiar words had brought comfort while the scent of well-loved pages had soothed her errant emotions after the incredible events of the morning.

Reading had also provided a distraction from the way her lips still burned from his kiss. The way her body still tingled in places it shouldn't after she'd nearly let him undress her on the deck of a boat in the middle of the sea.

"It's open."

The door swung open. He stalked into the room, his steps almost silent. Yet the energy he brought into the room, the sheer power that filled up every corner, made her breath catch. It took every ounce of willpower to stay where she was propped up with a mound of pillows at her back.

"When were you going to tell me?"

Her fingers tightened on the pages. Her hour of reckoning had come.

"Julius—"

He moved to the edge of the bed, his large frame looming over her.

"You put yourself in harm's way, Esmerelda."

Her mind screeched to a halt.

"Wait…what are we talking about?"

"I saw the video." He turned away and began to pace her room like a restless wild animal prowling about a cage. "You pushed me out of the way."

The parade. She stifled a groan. The event had gotten some minor attention on the international circuit.

"I was doing my job."

"By putting yourself in danger?"

His voice vibrated with anger and pricked her own temper.

"I believe the definition of a bodyguard involves some-

thing akin to that, yes. More of a focus on serve and protect, but protect does imply—"

"Parar."

He stopped in front of her window, hands on his hips,
his shoulders rising and falling with his ragged breathing.
Her ire cooled as she recognized that this was not a man
chastising her for doing her job.

She laid her book down and slid off the bed. She walked
up behind him. Slowly, she laid a hand on his back, felt
the tension bleed away at her touch.

"I'm all right."

He turned then, grabbed her hand and held it in his.

"The horse came down on your chest."

"Yes."

"Show me."

She knew what he meant, hesitated only a moment before pulling aside the neckline of her shirt. His eyes ze-
roed in on the half-moon scar just below her collarbone.

"I watched the video." His fingers came up, rested on
the white marking. The intimacy of it, of him touching
such a vulnerable part of her, stole her breath. "You didn't
hesitate."

"I couldn't."

He whirled away from her.

"Do you always give yourself away so lightly, Miss
Clark?"

Fury climbed up her spine, radiated throughout her
body.

"It was my choice and don't you dare question it."

"Choice," he spat out as he turned back to her. "Except
just this morning you told me you followed this path to
please your father. You sacrificed your own body to shield

me. And why? For duty? For a man who apparently cared for nothing but his job?"

"It's not just a job," she snapped back. "You told me countless times you and your father were the crown. There was no Julius without the title. It wasn't a matter of pride or ego, it simply was. You took your responsibilities and duties seriously, not because it brought you esteem or satisfied some selfish pleasure, but because you knew you could do it and do it well. There were times I saw how tired you were, how you wanted to step back, but you always moved forward."

"Moved forward at the expense of building relationships with others. I've read countless articles," he said at her confused look, "scoured TV and magazine interviews. Did you know I rarely talk about my mother? Don't even mention her. I can remember her, how much she loved me, and yet all I talked about was elections, construction projects, deficit spending. Even in that video of you..." He paused, looked down and sucked in a breath. "My father is king. He smiled at people, waved. I looked hard. Cold."

Her heart broke then, but in an altogether different way from when Julius had dismissed her. This time the fractures were for the man standing in front of her, a man torn between past and present, between the duty he had forgotten and the man he was without the burden of the crown.

"You could be, yes."

"Why?"

She shook her head.

"I don't know. I tried asking a few times after the accident."

"Why then?"

She hesitated. This was what came from telling lies.

One lie led to another, forced her to pause and think about what she was going to say.

Or you could just tell him now.

She looked up at him, at the tension furrowing his brow, at the pain and anger and fear lurking in his eyes.

No. Telling him now would be unburdening herself to get the weight of her own mistakes off her shoulders. Selfish. Adding to his conflict.

"We became closer after the accident." She would stick to the truth as much as possible. "You visited me in the hospital. You brought me a book. After that you started talking to me more, asking my opinion about legislation or something similar from a citizen's perspective."

"You said before we became friends."

"We did." She smiled sadly. "It was a very nice time in my life. I made friends at the academy."

"Like Burak?"

"Yes," she answered truthfully, despising the little flare of satisfaction at the jealousy in his voice. "Him and a few others. But after all the training, the last thing we wanted to do at the end of the day was talk more politics. Grabbing a drink at a pub, going sailing, watching movies. When I talked, you listened. You told me…"

Her tongue suddenly felt thick, her eyes hot.

"Told you what?" he prompted softly.

"You told me I made you a better leader."

It had been two weeks before Paris. How many times over that year had she caught him looking at her, wondered if he felt something more? As many times as she'd dismissed her thoughts as foolish, the naïve emotions of a love-starved young woman with a handsome, dynamic man for a boss.

But that day, after he'd asked her opinion on an email

he'd drafted to an ambassador regarding a recent disagreement they'd engaged in and she'd made suggestions to soften his tone, to offer an olive branch and maintain the relationship, he'd looked at her and smiled just enough to make his whiskey eyes crinkle at the corners.

"You make me a better leader, Clark. Thank you."

When she'd stuttered out *"You're welcome,"* his gaze had lingered, drifted down her body before returning to his computer.

And she'd known. Known the building attraction, the sensual tension she thought she'd imagined so many times, was not one-sided.

"And then I fired you."

Oh, God.

She closed her eyes. The way he'd done it had been awful. But the reason…oh, the further time moved away from that hideous day, the more she recognized that the reason itself was not wrong. If the roles were reversed, she wouldn't want a woman who had slept with her husband guarding him, being around them constantly. She could be angry, furious with him over how he'd done it.

But the reason made all the difference.

She opened her mouth to tell him, to let him know that there had been more than simple vanity or a royal's capriciousness behind his decision. He glanced over her shoulder and, before she could say a word, moved past her. For a moment, she thought he was going to leave. When his footsteps paused, she turned to see him standing next to her bed. Her chest tightened as he picked up her book off the bed, a dark green splash against the white feather comforter.

"Was it this book?"

"Yes."

He turned it over, his fingers lingering over the worn leather cover, the silver embossing on the spine.

"I remember it. I remember picking it up and thinking of you."

Her pulse thudded, slow beats that echoed in her ears. "Oh."

He set the book down on the bed and came back to her. His fingers brushed the material of her shirt to the side again, his eyes burning as he stared down at the scar.

"I never told you why I handled my duty from a distance? Placed a wall between me and my people, between me and everyone."

She shook her head.

"Whenever I tried to ask, you would change the subject or simply not answer."

His fingers drifted lower. His palm flattened against her chest, just above her breast, where her heart beat. A breath escaped him, as if he had needed to convince himself that she was still there, still alive.

"I'm sorry, Esmerelda."

She gave in to temptation and reached up, framing his face with her hands.

"No. Don't apologize. I'm the one who should—"

"Don't you dare." He caught her in his arms, his hands settling on her back and pulling her against him. "You pushed me out of harm's way."

"Yes, but that's not it. I—"

The words caught in her throat as he crushed his mouth to hers. This time she didn't hesitate. She moaned against his lips, her hands gripping his hair and pulling him closer. He swung her into his arms and carried her to the bed. Their mouths were still fused together as he lowered her to the soft surface, then covered her with his body. She arched against him, legs moving restlessly, nipples hardening as he continued to kiss her with reckless abandon. He pushed his hips against hers and she felt the hard length of his arousal against her core. She cried out.

"Esmerelda."

Her name came out on a guttural groan as he buried one hand in her hair, the other slipping up her side beneath her shirt, trailing over her stomach, before settling on her bare breast.

"Oh, Deus..." He lifted his head, stared down at her with eyes burning.

She blushed.

He grabbed the material of her shirt and pulled it up. Cool air kissed her breasts before his mouth descended, hot and wet, making her bow up off the bed as he sucked a nipple into his mouth and laved it with his tongue.

"Julius!"

He moved to the other, repeated the same tantalizing, delicious act of torture on her other breast. When she pulled at his shirt, he sat up and yanked it off before lowering himself back down. His bare chest pressed against her breasts. The intimacy of his skin naked against hers, the sheer heat of his body, sent a bold, erotic thrill through her. She reached up, her hands framing his face as she pulled his head down and pressed her lips to his.

More. God, she wanted more. Rational thought tried to break through, to remind her what she had been about to tell him. She needed to tell him before things went any further.

And then he pulled back. He stared at her, his chest rising and falling with heavy, ragged breaths. Embarrassment started to creep in.

"Julius—"

He rolled off the bed and stalked over to the window, hung his head and let out another harsh breath.

"I lost control. I'm sorry."

"Don't…" She fumbled, trying to come up with the right words. "Julius, I kissed you back—"

"I never should have come to your room in this state." He swore as he turned, his face shrouded in shadow. "I'm coming to understand I'm the sort of man who held himself back. Who kept things inside." He raked his hand through his hair. "And I lost control. Just like that."

He took one step forward, out of the shadows and into the golden glow of a lamp. Shock robbed her of speech as their eyes met. Desire burned, just as it had on the boat. But so did something else. Something she heard in his voice, felt in the way he'd touched her. Something that went deeper than simple lust.

Julius was coming to know himself once more. The past was merging with the present. Except this time, he still wanted her.

And I want him.

Before she could wrap her mind around what she'd been fighting the past few days, could accept that the man standing before her felt something similar to what she did, Julius moved past her toward the door.

"Wait!"

"Tomorrow, Esmerelda. We'll talk tomorrow."

The edge to his voice reminded her of the crown prince, authoritative and unyielding, his accent more pronounced. He was hurting, perhaps just as confused as she was.

She let him go.

The click of the door closing echoed in her room. Slowly, she sank into the embrace of her pillows. One hand drifted up, her fingers trailing over her swollen lips.

The last five minutes had been enlightening on multiple fronts. The question that had plagued her since he'd first appeared on the beach, however, remained the same.

What was she going to do?

CHAPTER ELEVEN

WAVES LAPPED GENTLY against the beach. Julius's bare feet sank into the wet sand, the ground cushioning his steps as the warm water swirled around his ankles before receding back into the ocean.

He needed this moment of peace before he went back to the villa. Needed the physical distance from the woman within its walls.

The memory of Esmerelda's body beneath his, her strong curves pressed against him, her passionate response as he'd tasted her body, made him hard almost instantly. Yet beneath the pulsing hunger ran a deep thread of guilt. While he couldn't remember his history with Esmerelda, he knew enough to know he'd hurt her deeply. The memory of her looking at him, her face stricken with hurt, as he'd determinedly pushed on with whatever he felt he'd had to say, haunted him. Yet twice yesterday he'd kissed her. Once where anyone passing by could have seen. Once in the privacy of her room where he'd pushed the boundaries even further.

Esmerelda had said they'd never been lovers. But something else had existed between them. An unacted-upon mutual attraction? Perhaps a plan to become something more, but he'd cut it short because of the engagement?

It was past time he and Esmerelda had a talk. He needed to know what had happened between them, needed to apologize for what other transgressions he had committed, before he could hopefully receive her forgiveness. Before they could move forward.

He reached into the pocket of his pants and pulled out the black box, flipping the lid open as he held it up. The diamond glowed, the freckles inside illuminated by the silver glow of moonlight.

The first time he'd held the ring, he'd thought of her. The idea of putting it on another woman's hand had him snapping the box shut and shoving it back into his pocket. Had he found some way for him and Esmerelda to be together? Was that a scenario she had ever entertained? Everything she'd said so far had suggested she hadn't wanted to be fired. But what about something more?

He followed the winding path back to the villa, his steps lit by sconces casting golden light onto the stepping-stones. The past kept them apart, as did their positions. He was the crown prince. She was his bodyguard. How could they explore their attraction if they never stepped away from their roles?

"Good evening, sir."

Julius looked up to see Aroldo on the terrace.

"Good evening." He nodded at the night sky. "A little late for you, isn't it?"

"Yes, sir. Doing my final rounds and then I'll be on my way. I will be gone tomorrow, so Michael will be attending to you and Miss Clark."

"Anything planned for your day off?"

Aroldo chuckled. "Hardly a vacation day. My daughter Hanna owns a rum distillery." Pride rang in his voice as he smiled. "She's hosting a masquerade gala tomorrow night to raise funds for our annual Spicemas carnival."

"A gala?"

"A bit fancier than many are used to. But Hanna is... strategic," Aroldo said. "Those not used to such affairs will enjoy themselves. Those who are will enjoy the food, the festivities, and hopefully donate."

An idea popped into his head.

"Is this gala open to anyone willing to make a donation?"

Aroldo's eyes narrowed. When he saw that Julius was serious, a conspiring twinkle appeared in his eye as he bowed his head.

"But of course, sir."

Satisfaction wound through him. A night to get away from the villa, to shed the titles of prince and bodyguard and simply exist as a man and woman, could only help. Not only could it lower the walls his past behavior and the difference in their stations had erected, but it would give Esmerelda a chance to indulge, to savor the moments she had so often been deprived of.

"Tell me where to send the money and it will be done within twenty-four hours. Esmerelda and I will be attending, although we'll be taking advantage of the masquerade to not reveal our identities to any of the guests."

"Of course, sir." The butler sounded faintly affronted that Julius would even suggest his betraying a guest's confidence. "I won't even tell my daughters." He looked down at Julius's bare feet. "I can procure you a suit and mask. I don't believe Miss Clark brought any evening wear."

Damn. Of course she hadn't. She thought she was going to be spending her days on a beach, not guarding her ex-boss or attending black-tie events.

He glanced down at his watch.

"It should be almost dawn in Paris. I'll have a special order arriving at the airport tomorrow in the early afternoon."

"It will be delivered the moment it arrives." Aroldo paused. "If I might, sir, my other daughter Joana is a seamstress. She has some creations that are suitable for the gala and that I believe would be to Miss Clark's liking."

"Anything you recommend."

Aroldo beamed.

"It will be done, sir."

As the butler hurried off, Julius smiled. He had no doubt that Esmerelda's first answer to his plan would be no, followed by a series of logical reasons as to why it wasn't a good idea. He formulated a list of responses as he entered the villa. The lights had been left on low, creating a golden glow that made the large space feel cozy and comforting. He turned the lights off as he walked down the hall. The moon shone bright through the skylights and lit his way.

He paused in front of Esmerelda's door. Temptation took hold of him, urged his steps closer. The memory of her—the taste of her skin, the music of her sharp cry as he'd kissed her breasts, the heat of her touch—filled him. He raised a hand to knock.

And stopped. If he knocked, if they picked up where they had left off, his physical desires would be satisfied. He had no doubt they would spend all night, if not most of the morning, enjoying each other's bodies. Exploring, savoring, delighting.

But the deeper yearning would still be there, the void in his memories rivaling the emptiness in his heart. He didn't just want Esmerelda in his bed.

He wanted her, all of her.

Slowly, he lowered his hand. Then he turned and walked down the hall, the thud of his footsteps mirroring the heavy beat of his heart.

Tomorrow.

He opened the door to his own room. A soft click sounded behind him. He looked over his shoulder.

All that greeted him was an empty hallway and Esmerelda's closed door glowing silver in the moonlight.

Esme sat at the kitchen island, her hands wrapped around a steaming cup of tea. Every sound, from the creak of a floorboard to the caw of a seagull, made her glance over her shoulder.

Where is he?

She'd laid on her bed for what felt like hours after Julius had left. One minute she'd decided to race after him, only to talk herself down the next. When she'd finally decided to find him, to tell him everything and lay bare not only their history but her desires, his room had been empty.

Both frustrated and relieved, she'd gone back to her room and sank into a hot tub. Not half an hour later she'd heard Julius and Aroldo on the terrace. She'd gone to fetch her robe, had been pulling it on when she'd heard his footsteps in the hall. Heard the pause outside her door.

Coward.

Her moment of bravery had evaporated beneath the twin weights of exhaustion and fear. She'd wanted him to knock, to open the door, to make the first move. To give her proof that she wasn't imagining things. To give her a much-needed dose of bravery to voice her wants.

And then he'd moved on. She'd opened her door just a crack, watched him move down the hall, before softly closing her door and sinking onto her bed once more.

Yet sleep had evaded her.

I want him.

So simple, yet so complicated. This time there was no underlying need for validation, none of the sycophancy that had overshadowed their first encounter. Then, there had been a sense of gratitude, that a man like him would deign to kiss a woman like her.

Unattractive. Unwanted. Unlovable.

Funny how one moment could wake someone up. Wake them up to the cold, hard truth that sometimes other people weren't right, they were simply awful. People like her parents, who had been so caught up in themselves and their own wants and desires that they hadn't bothered with their own child. People like the man Julius had been before, who had dismissed her so cruelly.

The seconds after she'd walked out of Julius's office had yanked her from that dark place where she thought she had to work more, do more, be more to be enough for others, and thrust her into the reality that whether she knew herself or not, she was enough.

A realization she had worked to accept over the past few weeks, along with exploring what she wanted instead of living her life for someone else.

And what she wanted, right now, was Julius.

In the span of a heartbeat, it had all fallen into place. She wanted Julius, wanted this complex man who had flown halfway around the world to seek her out. The desire she felt now didn't hinge on a need to be loved by someone else. It existed simply because she wanted it.

It was thrilling. Terrifying. It was still fated to end the way it had the first time; with them parting ways. But this time, it was on her terms.

As the shadows from the moonlight had shifted across

the silk covers, she planned. She would tell him everything. She would lay bare their past, tell him her wishes
now and place the choice at his feet. To have one last affair before he returned to Rodina and she continued on
with her new life. Or to part ways now with the memories, both good and bad, of who they had been and what
they had shared.

After I give him a piece of my mind about wandering off.

She'd slept until nearly ten in the morning and awoken to an empty villa. Panic had sent her running from
room to room. The housecleaning crew had already been
through, leaving behind fresh vases of flowers and polished floors in their wake.

But still no Julius.

What kind of bodyguard overslept and let her charge
wander out of her sight?

She'd called Julius. He'd sent her to voicemail. She'd
texted him. He'd told her Aroldo's son-in-law, a police officer, had a day off and was accompanying him on an er-
rand in town.

It hadn't been until Aroldo had arrived to prepare lunch
and confirmed not only that his son-in-law was with Julius but also a well-trained officer who was being generously compensated for his time that she had managed to
let herself breathe.

Julius had texted around noon, telling her that was she
was off-duty and the best thing she could do was relax.

She hated it. But unless she could somehow trace his
phone and call for a ride, she wouldn't be able to track
him down.

So she'd had lunch on the terrace, explored the villa's
library. She'd even spent an hour lying by the pool with a
book, forcing herself to try and relax as she waited for him.

It hadn't worked.

Now, with four o'clock fast approaching, she hadn't seen him all day.

Frustrated, she blew on her mug, watched steam curl up from the pink-tinted rose tea. Then stiffened as she heard footsteps coming down the hall. Her heart careened into her throat, butterflies flapping madly inside her chest as she sucked in a calming breath.

You can do this.

She turned just as Julius walked into the kitchen.

"Hello."

She bit back a flash of irritation at his casual greeting, strove for the same level of calm he exuded.

"Next time, I need to know where you're going and who you'll be with."

He stayed by the door, hands tucked into his pockets, his eyes moving up and down her body. Heat seared her fingertips as her hand tightened around the mug.

"Yes, Mom."

She narrowed her eyes.

"Your safety is not a joke."

His expression sobered.

"That was thoughtless. I'm sorry. I'm not used to the security and protocol. But Aroldo's son-in-law was both an excellent guard and guide."

"And generously compensated," she added dryly.

"That, too," he added with a grin that made her heart clench.

Now. Tell him now.

"I—"

"Would you like to go to a masquerade with me to-night?"

Her lips parted. Of all the things she'd anticipated him

saying, an invitation to a masquerade hadn't even made the list. "What?"

"A masquerade."

"But...where?"

"Aroldo's daughter Hanna operates a rum distillery near Grand Anse Beach. She's hosting a gala to raise funds for the island's annual Spicemas carnival in August. Aroldo compared it to the carnivals celebrated in late winter in countries like Brazil and the States."

"Oh." Mentally she started running through her checklist. "It's a little soon, but if I could get a copy of the floor plan, I could evaluate—"

He stepped closer, a slight smile lifting the corners of his mouth.

"Not as my bodyguard, Esmerelda. As my date."

Her mind slammed to a halt.

"Your date?"

Strange that the thought of going on a date frightened her more than going to bed with him. A date demanded more than a joining of bodies, more than a simple affair. It involved emotions and expectations. Was she prepared for something like this? Or would it cause old wounds to open, to lose the grip she had on her newfound confidence?

Before she could grasp onto a rational thought and think things through, he closed the distance between them, stopping inches away from her chair. His hand came up, his fingers gliding over her cheek, smoothing back a stray curl.

"We've been at odds since we met. Or at least since I first met you," he said with a small smirk. "Neither of us are denying the attraction between us. An attraction I suspect has been there for a long time."

She didn't deny, didn't look away. Not this time.

"But there's always something in the way. The past. Our

roles." He leaned down, his eyes heating as his hand slid into her hair. "Tonight, we're just going to be us."

Her chest rose and fell as she breathed deeply, tried to force herself to think past the desire humming inside her.

"And after tonight?"

God, she sounded wanton. Breathless. Husky.

"After tonight, the choice is yours."

She hesitated. "I believe that tonight it will actually become your choice."

A frown furrowed his brow. "Oh?"

"I want to talk...to tell you what happened between us. Before I left."

His face cleared. "I would like that, too."

"We could talk now—"

"One night, Esmerelda." He moved, brushed his lips across hers in a kiss so light it might have been the graze of butterfly wings. "One night of enjoyment, of just being two people on a date. Just us." Another kiss had her rising up to deepen the kiss, only to be thwarted when he released her and stepped back. "Then we'll talk."

"Okay." She released a pent-up breath and nodded. "Okay. I'd like that." She glanced down at her T-shirt and shorts. "I've got a sundress or two that might work. Maybe Aroldo could recommend a store that has a shawl..." Her voice trailed off as she looked up to see Julius's smug expression. "What?"

"I got you something."

She followed him down the hall to her room, anticipation building despite her best efforts to keep calm. It had been ages since she'd received anything more than a card wishing her a happy birthday.

He opened the door and stepped back. With a curious glance at him, she crossed the threshold.

And stepped into a dream.

Beautiful dresses were draped over the bed, hanging from the chandelier, laid out over a chair. Dresses in colors her mother had always warned her off from because it would be "too much" with her hair, her freckles. Gowns bedecked with jewels, garments fashioned from silk, dresses with yards of tulle that made her think of a princess from her favorite childhood fairy tale.

She had never cared much for clothes as a child. Barefoot had been her preferred shoe, shirts and pants she could get dirty her favored clothing. Her mother had foisted pretty dresses on her with warnings to sit still. For the longest time, Esme had associated quality clothing with being bored. By the time she had graduated college and started showing an interest in wearing something other than casual wear, she had been entering the academy, where her options had been limited to the three uniforms they wore during training, followed by black suits with white shirts once she'd landed her job.

Right now, though, as her fingers reached out and brushed over satin the color of a spring morning sky, she realized she liked pretty dresses very much.

"Julius...they're lovely."

He moved behind her, his hands settling on her shoulders. Her eyes grew hot as she looked down at her feet.

"But?"

"They're not...me." She swallowed hard and forced out a chuckle. "I can run two miles in just over thirteen minutes and ranked first in marksmanship. Can you really picture me in one of these?"

"In and out."

A shiver danced down her spine at the heated promise in his words.

"Julius…"

"Tonight isn't just about us, Esmerelda." He leaned down, his breath warm on her ear. "It's about you getting a chance to breathe. To enjoy yourself the way you had planned to before I crashed your beach."

"You mean before I trounced you?"

Her words died on a breathy moan as he nipped her earlobe.

"Minx." Before she could respond, he moved to the dresses laid out on the bed. "I had a dozen flown in from Paris this afternoon, although a few were made here on Grenada." He reached for a blue gown. "This one was made by Aroldo's other daughter Joana." He grinned at her. "Are you really prepared to tell Aroldo you didn't even try it on?"

A sense of breathlessness overtook her as Julius held up the gown. The bodice, fashioned from satin, featured a V-neck cut that flirted with the edges of propriety. Pale blue blended into midnight at the waist, a tumble of color that reminded Esme of day turning to night. It swept down into frothy folds of chiffon. Some of the material had been attached to the straps at the back and hung down to form cuffs fashioned out of the same dark blue and threaded with silver.

"It's stunning."

She glanced at herself in the mirror. At her toned arms and smaller bust, her mass of curls and freckles upon freckles.

But then she remembered the swing on the beach. When Julius had looked down at her and smiled and asked if she liked to swing or not.

Find out.

Did she like wearing beautiful dresses? Yes, she still

preferred being outside, being in the water or by the ocean. She loved walking in the sand, through the terraced vineyards in the fall and feeling the grass brush against her bare feet like velvet before the weather turned too cold.

Yet a part of her that was slowly coming to life wanted a touch of luxury, to feel confident in something other than her job. To feel beautiful.

She released a pent-up breath.

"I'll try it on." She let out a soft laugh. "I almost feel like Cinderella getting ready for a ball."

"Does that make me the fairy godmother?"

"I'll buy you a magic wand," Esme promised with a smile as she accepted the dress. "But it may not even fit."

"One way to find out." He caught her elbow, kissed her on the forehead so sweetly it made her throat tighten. "I'll leave you to make your selection. Meet me at eight in the main room."

She waited until the door closed behind him before she sagged.

Can I do this?

Yes, she wanted to tell him everything, to have no more secrets between them. Yes, she wanted to be with him again, to make love one last time.

And yes, she wanted tonight.

She shucked off her clothes and pulled the dress on, the luxurious blend of satin and chiffon whispering over her skin. She could feel the pull of temptation. Not just to wear an elegant gown, to play at being a princess for an evening, but to have a night with Julius in public. Yes, they'd be wearing masks. But it would be the first, and last, time she could simply enjoy being with him in front of others, without keeping her face schooled into a polite mask, mentally evaluating her actions and trying to keep her focus on Julius the job, not Julius the man.

She pulled up the zipper, although it only came up to her waist. Aside from the wide straps and the swaths of fabric that billowed beneath her arms, her back was bare.

She turned. And gasped.

The woman staring back at her from the mirror was someone she'd never seen before. The blue brought out the red gold of her hair, enhanced it. Instead of patterns and designs clashing with her freckles, the simple color scheme had her appreciating her speckled skin.

For the second time in her life, she felt beautiful. The first time had been when Julius had laid her back on his bed and gazed at her naked body. He hadn't said a word, but the appreciation blazing in his eyes had spoken volumes.

This time, however, as she grabbed the skirt and swished back and forth like a little girl, she felt beautiful all by herself.

Isn't there something magical in that?

CHAPTER TWELVE

JULIUS GLANCED AT his watch. Just after seven and the sun had already set. The drive from the villa to St. George's would take some time, although from what Aroldo had said, the festivities would continue well into the night.

There was no reason to rush. No specific event to get to. But every passing minute increased the tension tightening his neck, the unease in his gut.

What if she decided not to go? This afternoon she had seemed…at peace. A touch of playfulness that had stirred his blood, a hint of shyness that had made him want to gather her close and protect her.

Except what if he was pulling her close only to push her away? To hurt her once more?

He moved to the edge of the villa's grand hall. The missing pieces of his past were slowly falling into place. Along with the answers, though, came the realization that while he had been committed to his role as a leader, he had been a lonely and personally unhappy man. One who eschewed personal connections, buried himself in work. His mother's passing had buried him until he could barely breathe. Evading the ache, burying the sadness, had been his only answer. Avoiding grief from what had been, grief from what could be.

Never thinking about what the opposite of grief could be. Never allowing himself the indulgence of hope. Would the man he'd been, the one who kept his mind focused and his heart hard, accept the changes he was making now?

You saw me that day...

When she had uttered those words last night, the pain in her voice had nearly undone him. He'd hurt her so deeply she'd fled the country she loved. She'd told him they hadn't been lovers. But they had been something more than prince and bodyguard. Tonight, he would have answers.

He leaned against a pillar and stared out over the dark sky. How would this night end? Would she be able to let go at the gala, to see him as the man instead of the royal heir? Would he be able to accept what she had to tell him?

And perhaps the weightiest question of all, the one that hurtled him toward yet another unknown: where would it all lead?

"Hello."

The tension in his neck eased. He turned and froze.

Framed between two white pillars, she looked stunning. She'd left her hair unbound and flowing, wild curls tumbling over her shoulders. The dress clung to her breasts, followed the curve of her waist and then flared out into volumes of skirt. When she moved, the fabric parted to reveal a long, slender leg.

"Deus me ajude."

She smiled at him, a smile that caught him both for its beauty and its confidence. It was a smile he hadn't seen on her before. It lit up her face, her eyes crinkling with a pure happiness that attracted him both body and soul.

"Thank you. Julius."

Her use of his name heated his blood. He waited until she was just in front of him. He held out his hand, noted her slight hesitation before she placed her hand in his. He pulled her against him, watched as her lips parted, nearly gave in.

But he simply leaned down and brushed a kiss against her cheek. Surprise and disappointment flashed across her face before she could conceal them.

"You're welcome."

A car whisked them away to the distillery, perched on a low cliff near the white powdery sands of Grand Anse Beach. Golden light poured from the massive windows as men and women dressed in everything from glamorous evening wear to more festive costumes walked up a cobblestone pathway. Terra-cotta flowerpots lined the walkway, filled with magenta-colored bougainvillea and tall stems dripping with white amaryllis blooms.

The car stopped in front of the walkway. Julius slipped on his plain black mask and turned to Esmerelda. He held out his hand.

"Ready?"

She slipped on her mask, pale blue and trimmed with pearls, then accepted his hand. His fingers closed over hers.

"Ready."

The interior was stunning, with dark glistening floors, pale walls, and café lights draped across the ceiling. The distillery itself was on display behind giant windows that allowed guests in the event space to witness the process of manufacturing rum. Waiters in crisp white shirts and linen pants carried around silver trays with bubbling flutes of champagne, rock glasses filled with rum and a variety of cocktails. White tables carried bowls of Barbados and Caribbean lilies in vivid shades of pink and orange. A band sat on a raised dais at the far end of the room. Banjos, guitars and steelpans backed up the deep voice of the lead singer as his melodious voice drifted over the crowd against an upbeat song.

"The singer is Aroldo's nephew," Julius said in Esmerelda's ear as he led her toward one of the buffet tables. "His calypso band will compete in the Spicemas festival." He nodded to a tall round display. Small bowls were artfully arranged with flickering candles in between, each filled with spices, from the vivid yellow of turmeric to the tiny clusters of cloves. "The name is a nod to Grenada's spice production."

She glanced around the crowd. He could practically hear the gears turning in her mind.

"There's a lot of people here."

He nodded toward a man standing near the door. "Aroldo booked several private guards for the evening."

A reluctant smile appeared beneath her mask. "Am I that predictable?"

"Yes." He leaned down, unable to resist a taste of her lips. "Enjoy, Esmerelda. Something tells me you deserve indulgence."

They accepted glasses of champagne and found a seat in the corner. The music transitioned into reggae as more guests streamed into the building. A woman with Aroldo's dark blue eyes circulated among the tables, inviting people to tour the distillery.

"Would you like to go?"

Julius glanced at Esmerelda, saw her glance shift to the machinery behind the glass.

"No. But," he added as she started to sit back in her chair, "you should go. You're here as a guest, not a bodyguard."

Her lips, painted a sparkling caramel, turned down at the corners.

"It feels...wrong."

"But it's not."

The air changed between them, became charged with suppressed feelings: desire, vulnerability, passion.

A tall, willowy woman approached the table. Her hair, black and thick, had been wound into an intricate braid atop her head. The scarlet hues of her dress made her dark brown skin glow. She smiled at them.

"I'm Hanna, the owner of the distillery. You must be the mystery guests my father invited."

"Perhaps," Julius replied with a slight smile.

"Welcome. I appreciate you supporting our island." Hanna nodded to Esmerelda's dress. "I'd recognize my sister's handiwork anywhere."

Esmerelda laughed softly. "Touché. It's stunning. She could sell anywhere in the world she wanted to."

"I hope one day she will get the confidence to do so." She gestured to a small crowd gathering by the door that led into the distillery. "Would you like to join us for a private tour?"

"She'd love to," Julius answered before Esmerelda could decline. He felt her irritation, her sideways glance. But she rose and followed Hanna. A quick survey of nearby tables revealed more than one set of male eyes on her departing form.

His jaw tightened. Hard to be caught between the pride and happiness at seeing her feel as beautiful as she looked to him while wanting to lock her away where no other man could ogle her.

He stood and walked back to the spice display. Other small round tables in varying heights carried similar exhibits, from elaborate masquerade masks from the Spicemas carnival to pictures of the devastation a hurricane had wrought less than twenty years ago.

As he read, learned of the struggles faced by the island nation, the slim threads of responsibility that had been emerging with every recovering memory strengthened. As he saw the crowds of people sitting outside homes reduced to nothing but rubble, read of the challenges still faced by such loss, the threads knitted themselves together into something he recognized in the look he'd glimpsed on his own face as he'd read news articles, social media posts and blogs.

Duty. Obligation. Allegiance.

The sheer weight of it pressed on him, warred with how he felt about Esmerelda. Before his memories had started to return, before his present self had begun to merge with his past, she had been his focus.

But now…now he felt the pull, felt what the role of prince meant. Had he fought this battle before? Had he been a coward and simply given up? Or worse, had his former self discovered something he hadn't yet? That in order to carry on leading a country, he had to give up the one thing he wanted?

Fingers threaded through his. The pressure that had begun to build in his head eased as he looked down at their joined hands.

"Aroldo told me there are still struggles. He said a hurricane took out almost all of the buildings on the island. That was twenty years ago." She nodded toward the nutmeg seeds resting in the bowl. "One tree can take up to ten years to be fruitful."

"Generations lost in hours." He shook his head slightly. "It makes my current plight seem inconsequential."

She gave his hand a gentle squeeze. "But they haven't given up."

"No." He nodded at one photo that showed dozens of sailboats piled together like an angry child had scooped them up from the ocean and dumped them on top of one another. "It hits different. Seeing where the country is now, the work they've done, the work that still needs to be done."

"You're questioning yourself."

"Yes."

She leaned in. That floral scent that had been taunting him since the day he'd pulled her from the water wrapped around him. Orchids, perhaps, or some other exotic flower, touched with hints of vanilla and ebony. Sexy yet sweet. A scent that teased at one of the memories that had grown clearer but still lurked just beneath the surface of his consciousness.

"That makes you a good leader, Julius."

A satisfying warmth spread throughout his body. Not once had Esmerelda ever voiced anything but support for him as a leader, even as he doubted and questioned. That she continued to maintain her belief in his abilities, despite whatever had happened between them, touched him.

He brought her hand up and brushed his lips across her knuckles as the offbeat rhythms of reggae transitioned into a sultry, dark jazz.

"Dance with me."

Her eyes widened behind her mask.

"I can't."

"Can't or won't?"

That telltale flush crept up from the bodice of her dress, spread over her décolletage and moved up her neck.

"What if someone recognizes you?"

"Now you're making excuses." He leaned down, his

lips a breath away from her ear. "You want to dance with me, Esmerelda. So do it."

He heard the catch of her breath. Savored the soft exhale.

"All right."

He led her out onto the dance floor. He laid one hand on her waist and cradled her fingers in the other. The music sank beneath his skin. He pulled her closer, rested his cheek on her silky curls, cherished the feel of her in his arms. They drifted in and out of the other couples. The world blissfully faded away, leaving just the two of them in each other's embrace.

"Esmerelda…"

She relaxed against him, her trust meaning more than he could express.

"Yes?"

Her voice, low and gravelly, heated his blood. An invitation rose to his lips, to ask her to stay with him tonight. One hand glided up her back to draw her closer. His fingers brushed a raised scar on her back. He'd forgotten last night that the horse had first kicked her in the back when she'd shoved him out of the way. His throat tightened. He started to say something, to thank her, to chastise her, he wasn't sure.

But the words disappeared as he heard a horse's frightened whinny echo in his head, screams, wince as he felt the sharp scrape of gravel on his hands.

And the swift, stark fear.

He saw it then, a memory as real as his surroundings. Esmerelda's face twisted in pain, her eyes seeking out his face as he knelt beside her. The tiny smile of relief before her eyes rolled up and her head lolled to the side. He remembered the ride to the hospital, insisting on riding with her in the back of the ambulance. Pacing inside a private waiting room for hours before finally being allowed into her hospital room. Walking in and seeing her so pale beneath the freckles, her attempt to salute. Something inside him had come to life, as if it had been straining for years against the chains he'd bound around it and finally broken free.

Behind that memory, another rose.

He lifted red curls off her back, felt his throat tighten at the sight of the half-moon scar on her shoulder blade. For the first time in years, he surrendered to his emotions and pressed a soft kiss to the scar. The one she had sustained for him...

Julius reared back.

"Julius? What is it?"

So strange, how the different memories came back. Some felt like whiplash, whereas others trickled in.

This memory, the night he had raised a hand to her face, had cradled her as she'd leaned into his touch and accepted what he had offered, simply appeared, there all along waiting for him to open his mind to what he had shared with this woman.

This woman who, when he had asked if they had been lovers, had looked him in the eye and told him no.

Heat drained from his body, replaced by a chill that filled his chest.

"You lied."

CHAPTER THIRTEEN

THE MUSIC STOPPED. A loud bang sounded from the direction of the beach, followed a moment later by an explosion of red, green and yellow sparks visible through the glass panels in the ceiling. Gasps and excited exclamations circled through the room. Guests moved en masse toward the doors that led out onto a large stone terrace overlooking the sea.

The world around them moved. But Julius and Esme stood frozen in place, until they were the only two left in the room.

Only through sheer will did Esme manage to control her breathing and keep it from coming out in short, frantic gasps. Only through resurrecting the walls she'd built to shield herself against her parents' constant disappointment did she manage not to cave at the naked hurt in his eyes.

"Julius—"

"Not here."

He walked around and stalked across the room. She followed, her chin raised, shoulders thrown back. Yes, she had some mistakes to answer for. But damn it, she would not let him paint her as the villain of their story.

He waited until they were in the limo and the partition was raised before he spoke.

"You lied."

His voice was calm, cool. Yet beneath it she heard something that broke her heart. Hurt. She'd been so frightened those first few days of being hurt again, of reliving her own pain, that she hadn't bothered to think through the repercussions of what her lie would do.

"Yes."

"I asked you if we had been lovers. You said you had been my bodyguard and a friend."

"We had sex. We were not lovers."

He turned his head to look at her then, his face impassive.

"Is that how you excused it? With semantics?"

Tired of hiding, she tugged at the ties on her mask and pulled it off. "I knew what we had would never go beyond an affair, accepted it. But I at least thought you cared." She kept her voice steady. "I told you how important my job was, how it had become the only thing in my life that I was proud of. You took that from me without a discussion, without any courtesy for what I wanted. My parents did that. You did that. It hurt almost as much as how you dismissed me after what we'd just shared." She sucked in a deep breath. "I told myself that because love was never a part of what we had that we weren't lovers. But it was just an excuse. I lied. I'm sorry."

He stared at her for so long she wondered if he'd even heard her. Then he turned his head and looked out his window into the night.

"As am I, Esmerelda, for hurting you."

The villa came into view, a jewel bathed in golden light against the backdrop of a Caribbean night.

Julius pressed the intercom button. "Stop here, please."

The car stopped halfway up the winding drive.

"The car can take you back to the villa. I need a moment."

Julius got out and walked down toward the beach. Esme waited for all of three seconds, then got out and followed.

He stopped on the beach, one hand in his pocket, his mask hanging from the other by its ribbons. Lightning lit up the horizon in the distance, briefly highlighting where sky met sea. Then it disappeared and everything turned to midnight once more.

"I wanted to talk this afternoon." She stopped next to him. "To tell you everything."

Thunder rumbled, low and deep, rolling across the waves and up over the beach. The inner child in her who had curled up in her bed beneath a blanket to hide urged her to run back to the villa. The warrior she'd become anchored her feet in the sand and stood tall.

"You did. I'm not angry with you. I was, initially." He glanced down at her. "I'm mostly angry at myself. I knew there was something more between us."

She swallowed hard. "There was. We cared about each other, especially after my accident. At least..." She hesitated, then blazed forward. "I thought we did. I thought there was some affection between us."

"I still don't remember most of that year yet. Or my firing you. I just remember that night in Paris."

Her lips twisted. "Of course. The sex was good."

"More than good." His voice deepened, came out almost on a growl. "You know that as well as I do. It was incredible."

"It was. I like you, Julius. I admired you before, respected you. That was enough to get me into your bed. But the man you've been these past few days, it's like the man you were always meant to be. The compassion and kindness I saw glimpses of when I worked for you just seem like a part of you. The prince you were would have attended the masquerade and donated money, considering it an investment in the community and a good public relations move. The man you are now took the time to listen to stories like Aroldo's."

He turned to face her then.

"What are you saying?"

Her hands came up to rest on his jaw, framing his face as she raised up.

"I want you, Julius. Whether it's just tonight or the rest of your time here, I want to be with you."

"And after?" He gripped her shoulders. "What happens when I return to Rodina?"

Fear fluttered to life. She pushed it away.

"Don't think about after." Her words were nearly swallowed up by a sudden howl of wind that ripped at her skirts. "For tonight, let's do what you said. Just be us." She leaned up, brushed her lips over his. "Be with me."

Thunder clapped as the wind strengthened, ushering in the scent of rain mixed with the salt of the churning sea.

Then he leaned down and kissed her.

CHAPTER FOURTEEN

DOUBTS FLED AS Julius plundered her mouth. His lips sought as he explored her, tasted her. She moaned, her lips opening to him. He took everything she offered and demanded more. One hand cupped the back of her head, urged her closer.

Raindrops fell, the coolness a stark contrast to the heat inside her.

"As romantic as this is," Julius said with a carefree grin that made her breath catch, "I think a change of scenery is in order."

He swept her up into his arms and started up the stairs. The rain fell harder, drenching them both. She leaned back, tilted her head and laughed. When she looked back at Julius, he was staring at her as if he'd never seen her before.

"What?"

"That's the first time I've heard you laugh. Truly laugh." His hold on her tightened as he walked into his room through the terrace door. He set her on her feet, keeping his hands on her waist as he pulled her flush against him. "You're stunning when you laugh."

She kissed him, pouring all of her love and passion into it as she ran her hands up his back. He responded in kind, his primitive growl thrilling her as lightning lit up the room. He kept her cradled in his arms as he stood and crossed to the bed. He set her down gently, grabbing her hands in his and lifting her up to her knees.

"Don't move."

She watched him as he advanced, the lightning casting shadows over his masculine face that made him seem even darker, more dangerous. Before, in Paris, it had been sweet and soft, romantic, yet at times distant, as if Julius had been holding a part of himself back.

Here, now, she saw everything. More thrilling, and more terrifying, he let her, showing her his hunger, his desire.

His fingers slid under the hem of her blouse. Up and over her head, leaving her clad only in a strapless bra. His hands slid up her naked waist, around her back. The material fell away. Suddenly shy, she resisted the urge to cover herself.

"Beautiful." Julius stared down at her as if he couldn't believe she was real. "So beautiful, Esme."

One arm wrapped around her waist. A moan escaped her lips as he bent his head and sucked the tender tip of her breast into his mouth.

"Julius!"

His tongue flicked over the sensitive peak before he placed soft kisses on her breast before moving to the other. The strength of his arm wrapped around her anchored her as the sensations of pleasure spread from where his mouth made love to her body, filling her with a liquid warmth that made her limbs heavy even as it made her chest feel light.

Emboldened by his touch, she placed her hands on his chest and pushed back.

"My turn."

Fire flashed in his eyes. Slowly, he sat on the edge of

the bed next to her. She undid the buttons on his shirt one at a time, her breath catching as she unveiled his muscular chest. At last, she pushed the shirt off his shoulders and placed her lips to the skin over his heart.

She rose up once more on her knees, looped her arms around his neck and pressed her body against his. The dark curling hair on his chest rubbed against her breasts, the coarse contrast sending an erotic shudder through her body. She bowed her head and kissed the pulse beating at the base of his throat.

Before she could continue her exploration, he shifted, rolling and pinning her to the bed.

"Not fair!" she cried out with a laugh that turned into a groan as he licked one breast.

"You can play more next time."

He moved down her body, trailing kisses down her stomach as his hands made quick work of her skirt and underwear.

"Next time?" she finally managed to say as his hands gripped her thighs.

"Next time," he repeated firmly. "You have memories of us, memories of a night in Paris. I have nothing but a few flashes of dreams. And now," he said with a wicked smile that made her feel like the devil himself had caught her in his grasp, "I want to make those dreams a reality."

He lowered his head. Her hands fisted in the sheets as he kissed the insides of her thighs, gently nipped her flesh. When he placed his mouth on her, she bowed up off the bed into his caress, a sharp cry escaping her lips. He pressed her back down and held her firm as he licked, kissed and sucked, at times gentle and sweet, other times with a passionate finesse that left her breathless and restless.

Suddenly, she felt her body shift. Tiny bits of electricity began to build inside her body, pulsing as one as they rushed to the center of her body.

"Julius," she gasped, "Julius, I'm… I'm going to…"

She shattered. Pleasure careened through her body, spiraling out and lighting every nerve on fire before leaving her weak and trembling.

Dimly, she felt the bed shift beneath her. She opened her eyes to see Julius removing his pants. She watched, unashamed, as he straightened and stood completely naked before her. He'd lost weight, yes, but he was still as she remembered. Broad shoulders narrowing down to a tapered waist, a chest and arms kept muscled by rowing, horseback riding and sparring.

Her cheeks grew warm as her gaze trailed down to his hips and his hard length. Heat suffused her body as he reached down and wrapped his hands around himself.

"You do this to me, Esme."

Feminine satisfaction curled through her.

"Should I apologize?"

His lips quirked up as he stalked closer to the bed.

"No."

He reached into the drawer of the bedside table. After he was sheathed in a condom, he moved back onto the bed. He gently pushed her back into the pillows. She lay there, waiting, watching his gaze roam over her. The longer he looked, eyes pausing on freckles here and freckles there, the more some of her desire started to slip away, replaced by the ugly tuggings of self-consciousness.

"Beautiful."

He covered her body with his, tangling his hands in her hair and kissing her hard once more. With the evidence of how much he wanted pressed against her hips, her doubts receded, replaced by embers that grew into flames.

Flames that licked at her skin as he slowly slid inside her body.

"Julius!"

"You feel so good, Esme." He buried his face in her hair, inhaling her as if he would die without her. "So good."

Their bodies found a rhythm, moving against each other, climbing higher, soaring toward the highest peak until she crested once more. He followed a moment later on a groan, shuddering against her.

After, he rolled to the side but kept his arms around her waist, pulling her closer until her back was flush against his chest.

"Don't go."

She closed her eyes for a moment. He'd said almost the same words before in Paris. Her heart clenched at the reminder that, no matter what this was between them, it would never result in a happily-ever-after.

So say yes now.

"I'm not going anywhere."

Not yet.

CHAPTER FIFTEEN

JULIUS SAT IN a lounge chair by the window, the curved back cradling him as he watched the storm stir the sea into crashing waves, the peaks made jagged by wind that ripped across the ocean.

It was glorious in its fury. Lightning forked across the sky. For a moment, the Atlantic was lit by a brilliant white light that would have delighted even the most curmudgeonly of individuals.

Julius noted the beauty. The uniqueness of the landscape.

And found it wanting compared to Esmerelda.

She slept a few feet away on her stomach with the sheet pulled just up to her waist. His eyes slid over her bare back, the toss of curls that partially obscured her face, her arms clutched around a pillow.

He raised his glass to his lips, sipped the rich whiskey and savored the slight burn down his throat. She had asked for nothing more than tonight. How many men in his position would have been thrilled at a night of pleasure with no strings attached?

Yet a hard stone had settled in his stomach at the thought of only one evening, perhaps a few if he took her up on her offer of continuing their affair until he left Grenada. He didn't want this to be the end. There had been something there between them from the beginning of this whole adventure. Something that had made her, and only her, stay in his memory. The more he talked to her, spent time with her, the more he couldn't begin to fathom how his former self had let her walk out of his life.

His eyes drifted toward the wall safe hidden behind a painting of one of Grenada's waterfalls. Every time he thought of the ring, he thought of Esmerelda. He'd bought it for her.

But had he? What if he had wanted to, was experiencing the desires he'd silenced in order to fulfill his duty to his people?

He sighed and let his head drop back onto the chair. He'd reviewed the laws of Rodina, along with the marriages of the past five generations of royals dating back to the mid-eighteen-hundreds. The heir apparent had always been bound by expectations and the best interests of the country.

All his speculation brought him, repeatedly, back to the one truth he didn't want to face. He had not found a way to strike a balance between his duty to his country and his feelings for Esmerelda.

Another bolt of lightning dove down toward the churning sea. Thunder followed less than a second later, roaring as if to let the whole world know of its immense power. It rumbled across Julius's skin, a not unpleasant feeling, and slowly he let his eyes drift shut.

The dream came to him, vivid and detailed.

Esmerelda naked beneath him, her body dotted with freckles. He kissed them, each one that he could, thrilling at the throaty sound of her laugh.

"There's too many for you to kiss them all."

"I don't mind trying." He kissed one on the curve of her hip, savored the hitch in her breath as his lips trailed to the fiery red curls between her legs. *"Besides, we have all night. And as you like to point out, I'm very thorough."*

Her laugh turned to a moan, her fingers threading through his hair as he made love to her with his lips.

"Julius..."

His heart twisted in his chest. He'd been denying it for months, telling himself he was mistaking appreciation for something more.

But as he moved up her body and covered her with his own, he knew it wasn't indebtedness or gratitude. No, he—

"Julius?"

She sat on the ottoman opposite him. Possessiveness gripped him at the sight of her in his dress shirt, her long legs shown off to perfection. The glimpse of freckled thigh that nearly made him groan out loud.

"I'm sorry to wake you."

"It's all right." He held up his glass. "Care to join me?"

Her eyes flickered to the whiskey.

"Yes."

Surprised, he tilted his head to one side. When he reached out for her hand, she placed her fingers in his grasp without hesitation.

"Is everything all right?"

The storm nearly drowned out the sound of her soft sigh.

"Yes. Just...restless."

He held out his own glass. She took a sip, her eyes drifting shut as she made a noise of appreciation he felt all the way to his groin.

"What's wrong?"

Thunder clapped once more. She stood, rubbing her hands on her bare thighs as she moved over to the decanter.

"Do you mind?"

He stood and crossed to her.

"No. But seeing as you're my guest," he said with a soft kiss on her lips, "I'll get it."

He poured her a glass, watched her fingers tighten as she accepted it and took a healthy sip before moving back to the ottoman.

"Is it the storm?"

She waited a moment, then slowly nodded. "I used to be scared of them. Now they don't bother me if I'm awake. But if they wake me up, it takes a while to get back to sleep."

"What did you do to get over your fear?"

She stared down into her glass. "I just…did."

He frowned. "What about your parents?"

"My mother was usually out at some function or another. My father told me to be brave."

Anger surged through him.

"That's it?"

"That's it."

He set his glass down on the table next to his chair and held out his hand.

"Come here."

She stared at his hand. For once her emotions were transparent and vivid. Fatigue, weariness, embarrassment.

But what made his pulse pound and his heartbeat quicken was the naked longing in her eyes.

Slowly, she set her own glass down and stood. He held his breath, waited until she was right in front of him, before he clasped her hand in his and gently tugged her down onto his lap. She curled into him, her face falling against his neck as he wrapped his arms around her and let his breath rush out as his body shuddered.

Home.

The thought appeared unbidden. The word inspired no memories, no recollections of a house or a castle or some other place. But he knew its meaning, knew in that moment that home would be wherever this woman was, so long as she was by his side.

"You're safe."

She leaned back slightly, her lips just a breath away from his.

"I know. I'm with you."

The trust she placed in him, her surrender, rendered him speechless. He cupped the back of her head, kissed her with a gentleness that seemed to surprise both of them. His other hand drifted down, tugging at the buttons of the shirt she wore. Revealing her freckled beauty inch by inch until the shirt whispered to the floor.

Before he could move, she stood. Pushed him back into his chair and knelt before him.

"Esmerelda—"

She placed a finger over his lips. "I want this, Julius."

His protests died as her fingers slid beneath the waistband of his silk pants. She unveiled his hard length, her hands teasing, her smile confident and glorious as she lowered her head and took him in her mouth. He groaned, his hands sliding into her hair as she ran her tongue over him, kissed him, brought him to the edge of control.

Her throaty chuckle nearly undid him. She moved, rising above him like a flame-haired siren as she straddled his lap and guided him inside her wet heat. Her body closed around him as she placed her hands on his chest and started to move. His hands closed over her waist, guided her as she rode him.

Lightning flashed. Thunder crashed. They both soared

over the peak, her cries of pleasure mingling with his groan as she collapsed against him.

Julius awoke to sun streaming in through the windows and an empty bed. Unease sent a jolt of energy through him. He'd fallen asleep with Esmerelda in his arms, her face relaxed and content. Had she awoken and, satisfied with their one night, left? Or had she had second thoughts?

One way to find out.

He tossed back the covers and stood. He was in the process of pulling on a pair of shorts when the door to his room opened.

"Good morning."

Esmerelda walked into the room carrying two cups of coffee. With another sundress on, this one the color of bright lemons, her hair falling wild and untamed about her face, she looked relaxed. More herself, he realized with a satisfied smile as his apprehension slipped away. He accepted a mug and took a deep sip.

"I wondered where you were," he said. He leaned down and kissed her, satisfaction curling through him when she didn't pull away.

"I'm used to rising early," she said with a small smile. "Back in Rodina I had to get up at five a.m. in order to be ready for the day."

"Was that the time I set?"

"It was."

He grimaced. "Bastard."

She reached over and laid a hand on top of his.

"You owe it to your past self to give him a break. No, he wasn't the warmest and fuzziest of princes," she said with a small smile, "but he ruled and did very well for the people of Rodina."

"So you've said."

She stared down into her coffee mug, her sudden silence cluing him in that something was on her mind.

"What are you thinking?"

"One of the times I prompted you to take a break, you told me you couldn't. That there was work to be done. I said the work would still be there in five minutes." She looked at him then, sadness making the green of her eyes all the more vivid. "You said it would, but you might not be. That life was short and you had a duty to do your job while you could."

"My mother."

Just thinking of Elizabeth made his pulse pound in his throat.

"I believe so." Her hand settled on his once more.

They sat. Sadness permeated the air, but it wasn't unpleasant. It was healing, revisiting the memories he had reclaimed, finally allowing himself the chance to grieve as he suspected he never had.

"A conclusion I came to myself a couple days ago. I chose duty over grief. Logic over emotion."

"Understandable."

"For a time. But then it became comfortable. Easy." He squeezed her fingers. "I retreated into my indifference. It was cowardly."

"Cowardly." She echoed his word with a slight smile. "I was cowardly, too."

"How so?"

"I was very good at being a bodyguard. I'm active, I kept in good shape. I genuinely love Rodina, so serving in a role that helped me serve my country was appealing. But it also allowed me to put off examining my life. Figuring out what I wanted to do for me." She scoffed. "Isn't it awful that sometimes staying in the rhythm of past mistakes is easier than trying something new that could make you happier?"

"I did the same."

She looked at him then, her gaze thoughtful.

"Yes, you did."

A different type of intimacy settled between them. For the first time since he'd arrived, he felt as though they were seeing each other, truly, in all their beauty and faults. And still they sat side by side, content.

"Join me on the balcony."

She smiled and accepted his hand up. He kept his fingers wrapped around hers as they walked onto the terrace and settled at a bistro table by the edge. Aside from the glistening drops still clinging to the trees, there was no evidence of the storm that had battered the island the night before.

"What would you like for breakfast?" he asked.

"I've already had some fruit."

"Fruit is not breakfast," he replied. "You're on an island where you can have anything you want."

She glanced down, her cheeks turning red.

"That's one of the things I love."

Her head shot up, her eyes widening.

"What?"

"I can always tell your emotions by the color of your skin. For example, right now with that beautiful bright red and your cheeks like apples, I know you're embarrassed."

"Stuff it," she replied, her cheeks growing even redder.

"I also know," he added, his voice deepening, "that whenever you look like a rose, you're thinking about everything that we did last night."

A smile tugged at her lips.

"It is one of the curses of being a redhead."

"Not a curse." He paused. "It was one of the ways that I knew that there was more to our past relationship than what you were telling me."

He had mostly reconciled what had happened, the way she had manipulated the truth. But it lingered in the back of his mind. A conversation unfinished.

She glanced out over the ocean.

"I am sorry for that," she said softly. "It was never my intention to lie to you. It just…"

Her voice trailed off. Regret hit him as he remembered the pain in her voice when he'd first arrived. Her shock and pain.

"I'm sorry, Esmerelda. Unfortunately, that's all I know how to say now. I wish I could remember why. Could remember what I said."

Esme sighed.

"It was painful yes. But it was more how you did it, which we've already been over." She looked back down at her coffee. "I was embarrassed, too. I thought we had a little more time together. I thought that our affair was more than just a one-night stand. Not that I expected anything to come of it," she added quickly. "I always accepted that we were from different worlds. That you would have to eventually move on as I would. I just didn't expect for that to happen less than a week after we…" The rosiness returned to her cheeks. "After Paris."

"Why do you think it did? Truly."

"Your father is doing well for his age. But he's nearing seventy. He's been vocal about wanting to step down before he's seventy-five, perhaps sooner, and pass you the crown."

Julius's hand tightened around his cup. He could barely

wrap his head around being a prince. Now he might be a king in less than five years?

"Hence his encouraging me to get engaged."

"I believe so." She sighed. "I wouldn't want my husband's former lover still around. It was an understandable move."

Jealousy seized him at the mention of her phantom spouse. The thought of any other man touching her the way he had, saying vows to cherish and protect, having a family with her, made him want to hurl his mug at the wall.

"No, it wasn't."

"But—"

"No buts, Esmerelda. I treated you horribly after everything you did for me. Not just saving my life, but serving me selflessly for over a year." She opened her mouth, probably to utter another protest. "Don't let my slightly better treatment of you than how your parents treated you eclipse the fact that I handled things the wrong way."

Her lips parted as her eyes widened. She sat back in her chair, eyes blinking rapidly.

"Well," she finally said, "that was profound."

"And accurate."

"To a point." She held up a hand to silence his own protest. "One bad deed does not deserve another. I could have simply put you off instead of lying." She glanced out toward the sea, her expression turning pensive. "But it did help. I don't think I would have ever left if you hadn't given me a reason to."

"Do you think staying in Rodina would have held you back?"

"I'd like to think not. But I was always living my life for someone else. The love my parents offered me was conditional on doing what they wanted for me. What they thought was best." Her chest rose and fell on a soft sigh. "I didn't realize how much I needed to make a choice for myself until I was on that plane flying away." She turned back, her smile glowing. "I've already grown so much these past few weeks. Imagine what could happen next. I could be anyone I wanted to be. Not something someone else wants for me."

His chest twisted into a hard knot. The right thing to do was be happy for her, be glad that she had found purpose amidst pain. Yet as he looked at her, the confident tilt of her chin, the slight smile on her lips, all he felt was something dark and desolate, a hollowness that rivaled the emptiness in his mind.

He stood, set both their mugs on the table, and pulled her to her feet, indulging in a long kiss that seeped into his veins and banished the heaviness that had settled on his shoulders.

"What were you thinking you wanted for breakfast that made you blush?"

"Oysters."

He arched a brow. "Is that meant to be foreplay?"

She laughed. "No, I've just always associated oysters with vacations and indulgence."

"Did I eat them?"

"I don't know. I was paying more attention to the crowds and possible assassins instead of watching what you had on your plate."

He lightly swatted her on the rear for her impudent answer before swinging her into his arms, enjoying her gasp of surprise before he set her back in her chair.

"Well, I don't know if I enjoy them or not, but I'll try them."

He texted Aroldo. Fifteen minutes the butler brought

out a silver tray laden with eggs Benedict, fresh fruit, a variety of cheeses and in the middle of the tray a silver bowl with raw oysters on ice.

Aroldo glanced between the two of them, a small smile on his face as he set the table.

"Enjoy, Your Highness…miss."

He bowed his head and disappeared back into the villa. Esmerelda made a soft noise that sounded like a strangled laugh.

"Do you think he knows?"

"Yes."

"Oh, God." Her hands flew up and covered her face.

"He's seen far worse than some rumpled sheets, believe me."

"I know, but he seems so…fatherly. It's like getting caught naked."

"If you're suggesting we go back in and make love again, I'm all for it."

Her laugh trickled over him. "And ruin all of Aroldo's hard work?"

They dined on the eggs and fruit. Julius nearly choked on the first oyster he tried.

"It's slimy."

Esmerelda dipped hers in the small container filled with cocktail sauce and popped it into her mouth, her eyes drifting shut as she moaned.

"They're delicious."

"Slimy," Julius repeated.

"More for me, then."

He watched, amused and grateful to see her like this. Relaxed, joyful. Even though so much of his identity remained wrapped up tightly in his mind, even though their future together remained up in the air, he felt happy for the first time in his limited memory.

They spent the rest of the morning on the terrace by the pool, alternatively lounging in the chairs and swimming in the warm waters. A shower after lunch led to him wrapping her water-slicked legs around his waist and driving himself into her, her back pressed against the tiles, her mouth fused to his. The afternoon included a ride in a Jeep and a hike to a waterfall, where Esmerelda terrified and aroused him by jumping off a cliff into one of the pools. When he chastised her, she splashed him, resulting in a battle that ended with them laying on a stretch of sand behind the falls, kissing and running their hands over each other until they worked themselves into a frantic frenzy. They'd barely made it back to the villa before he'd carried her to his room and made love to her again.

Dinner was salad and a Grenadian stew, discreetly left under a tray on the terrace table with a note from Aroldo stating that he would return in the morning. They lingered over the wine, talked, savored each other's company and then savored one another's bodies once more as the sky darkened. They fell asleep once again wrapped in each other's arms.

It was around midnight when Julius awoke and remembered.

CHAPTER SIXTEEN

THE DIAMOND GLEAMED beneath the rosy light of dawn sweeping across the sea and up onto the terrace. Miss Smythe's words came back to him as he stared at the ring.

"The longer you look, the more you see."

It had always been for her. He remembered now, sitting in the elegant opulence of Smythe's, dismissing twenty-carat diamonds and pure red rubies.

And then he'd seen it. The salt-and-pepper diamond. The inclusions scattered inside had reminded him of her freckles, of how he'd kissed her in Paris and made her laugh.

The longer he'd looked at Esmerelda, the more he'd seen. She'd gone from being a highly rated graduate and an effective bodyguard to a flesh-and-blood woman he couldn't get out of his mind.

Her courage had humbled him. Her dedication had intrigued him. And the shy smile she'd shot him in the hospital after her accident when he'd given her something so simple—a book he'd somehow recalled her mentioning a week before the accident—had shot past years of defenses and grabbed hold of his cold heart.

He'd denied it at first. Chalked it up to an emotional reaction to her saving his life. But her actions had created an intimacy neither of them had expected. Instead of just issuing orders, they'd talked. He'd come to respect her opinions on Rodina, even if he didn't always agree with them, found himself looking forward to seeing her each day.

Then they'd gone to Paris. They'd traveled together before. But Paris had been the first time they'd had hours of nothing: no meetings, no press conferences or fundraising events. He'd stepped out of the hotel, away from the bodyguard on shift just to have a minute to breathe. Then he'd seen her at the café, head tipped back, curls tumbling down her back and freedom in her eyes as she'd soaked up her surroundings. It was as if the thin veil he'd purposefully pulled down between them had been ripped away. The feelings he'd barely kept at arm's length over the year had risen, overwhelming his resolve.

The longer I looked, the more I saw.

He reached out, laid a finger on one of the pearls circling the diamond. That night had been one of incredible pleasure. But it had also solidified the connection he'd felt growing between them. When she'd come to him the morning after on the balcony, her touch smoothing away some of his inner turmoil, he'd known that what he felt for Esmerelda had been much more than casual lust.

When his father had come to him on his return from Paris and brought up the need for an engagement, it had been a reprieve. He did well with orders, with facts and lists. But feelings, emotions…those hadn't factored into his life for years. As he'd made the arrangements for Esmerelda's reassignment, he'd kept himself numb, resolute against the occasional flicker of conscience or the annoying tug of his heart.

And then she'd left.

The ache came as swiftly as the sunlight spreading

across the sea. It had taken him days to acknowledge he missed Esmerelda, and several more before he made his decision. He'd told himself that Esmerelda was a good choice. Her loyalty to the throne, her dedication to the country, her vast knowledge of politics and government, were not the traditional assets of wealth, land and power brought by previous brides and grooms. But Rodina's economy was stable and strong. The entire island had been a part of Rodina for generations. And he and his father had both made significant headway in international forums.

All justifications he'd presented to his father a week after Esmerelda had left. Justifications his father had swept aside with one simple question.

"Do you want to marry her?"

Julius hesitated. He had never made a decision, let alone one so crucial, with emotions playing a pivotal role.

"Yes."

Francisco smiled. "Then what are you doing here? Go find her."

So he'd done it. He'd jumped in headfirst, digging the black card he'd been presented with by a reclusive billionaire out of his desk and flying to London while a private detective from England had tracked Esmerelda down and provided her address in Grenada.

And now he was here, with his memories intact and Esmerelda sleeping in the room behind him. Anticipation filled him. When she awoke, he would tell her everything. Then he would present the ring to her properly. They could be engaged for as long as she wanted, have whatever sort of wedding she desired.

So long as she was by his side, nothing else mattered.

* * *

Esme awoke to rays of morning sun warming her face. The bed was empty, but a glance at the clock revealed it was after eight o'clock. Julius had always been an early riser.

So had she, she thought with a satisfied smile as she stretched. Until she indulged in a passionate affair with a lover who knew her body better than she did and spent hours worshipping it.

"You're awake."

Julius walked in. He smiled and leaned down to kiss her. She sat up and raised her face to him. "Good morning."

"Good morning."

She frowned, trying to pinpoint his mood. There was an energy to his movements, bordering on uncontrolled, that seemed off. Yet there was also a touch of formalness in his face and tone that reminded her of the old Julius. A distance that couldn't be bridged, not even by the intimacy of the bedroom.

"I remembered."

She froze. "Remembered?"

"Everything."

She sat for a moment, waiting. But when he didn't look at her in disgust, when he still smiled at her, she smiled back, throwing back the covers to go to him.

"I'm happy for you, Julius."

She hugged him. He wrapped his arms around her, his hands a comforting warmth on her bare back.

"Wait…does that mean you remember what happened in London?"

He nodded, the light in his eyes dimming a fraction. "I was on my way back to the hotel. I heard a scuffle coming from an alley. Two men fighting. I went to break it up.

One ran off. The other turned on me and pointed a gun at my face."

Her entire body tightened.

"What?"

"He fired."

Fear clogged her throat.

"Julius…"

"Obviously something went wrong." His lips twisted into a slight smile. "The gun jammed. I lunged for him and we got into a fistfight. I remember pain," he said, touching the back of his neck, "and stumbling into the parking garage hotel. There was a private elevator entrance down there for the penthouse. The doors closed and that's all I remember."

"He must have mugged you."

"I called Scotland Yard. They're running searches on my credit cards to see if any have been used recently, and they're pulling CCTV footage from the area. I remembered everything about the week after we spent the night together in Paris. I remember our conversation when I told you that you were being reassigned."

Trepidation slithered up her spine. She had grown so much in just a few days. Could she handle what he had to tell her? Hear him, accept it and move on?

"Julius—"

"I was intentionally cruel."

She leaned back. "Why?"

"I wanted to make you hate me. I thought it would make it easier for you to move on. It wasn't right," he added. "I made a choice for you that wasn't mine to make."

Her eyes grew hot.

"Thank you, Julius."

"It feels like…" He looked at some distant point over

her head. "Like I've been put back together. Like all the pieces are there."

She forced a smile onto her face, trying to focus on his relief instead of her own selfish worry that in regaining his memory he'd lost a bit of the man he'd discovered here on the island.

"I remembered the ring, too."

Her stomach dropped. She'd known this was going to happen. Once again, it had come too soon. But she would handle it better this time.

"I see." She planted her hands on his chest and tried to push him back, but he held her fast. "I'm not comfortable standing here naked while you tell me about the ring you purchased for another—"

"I bought it for you, Esmerelda."

For a moment she couldn't breathe, could only stare up at him as the words repeated over and over in her head.

"What?"

"After you left, all I could think of was you. Just the thought of sharing dinner, let alone my life, was impossible."

He reached over and grabbed the black box off a side table. Her heart surged into her throat as he opened the box to reveal the ring nestled inside.

"Esmerelda, would you be my queen?"

Her hand flew to her throat. Never in her wildest dreams had she ever thought she and Julius could be together. Could have a life together. It almost seemed too good to be true.

Something tugged at her, a thread of reality pulling at the beautiful tapestry of dreams Julius had woven around them.

"Julius, I… I don't know what to say."

He frowned.

"Say yes. We can have as long of an engagement as you want. Whatever kind of wedding you want. And then we can be together. Rule together."

She stepped away, and this time he didn't stop her. She grabbed her robe off the floor and pulled it tight around her. When she turned back, he was watching her with a hooded gaze, his fingers clenched around the ring box.

She pushed her curls out of her face.

"Julius…it's very sudden."

"We've known each other over a year."

"Yes, in a professional capacity."

He ran a hand through his hair. "Would you prefer we date? Go public with a relationship first—"

"No."

Frustrated with herself, with him for springing this on her so suddenly after the roller coaster they'd ridden over the past week, she wrapped her arms around her middle and moved to the windows. She heard him move behind her, felt his presence at her back.

"What's going on, Esmerelda?"

"Why me, Julius?"

"What?"

She turned then, hated seeing the frustration and confusion on his face.

"Why do you want to marry me? Why, after dismissing me, did you change your mind?"

He reached up and cupped her face. She leaned into his touch, the same way she had in Paris, her heart teetering on the edge of hope and anguish.

"Because I realized you were the right choice. We work well together. We both love Rodina. We can do more for the people as a team than any of the women my father had listed. And he agreed. He supported my choice. But this was my plan for us."

Each sentence he uttered was a death knell to hope. How cruel was life to dangle such an incredible week in front of her, to tease her with intimacy and tenderness and newfound confidence, only to rip it away once more?

"I'm an asset in my own way, then."

He frowned. "It's not just that, Esmerelda. We care about each other. Genuinely care," he added, his emphasis on *genuine* making her nauseous.

"I need more than that, Julius."

His lips parted. But nothing was said.

Her heart gave one last, painful gasp. Then a shield dropped down, the same shield she'd used to utter her words of resignation and walk out of his office all those weeks ago.

"I see."

"Damn it, Esmerelda, I just regained my memory. I'm shirking generations of tradition because I want you as my wife."

"You didn't even ask me what I wanted." She stepped back. "If becoming your queen was what I wanted. You just assumed I'd jump at the chance. You planned everything without asking what I wanted."

"I told you, we can do the engagement and the wedding—"

"What about after?" she asked, repeating his words from the night when they'd stood on the storm-tossed beach. "After the pretty pictures and the walk down the aisle?"

"My father would abdicate one year after our marriage. I would become king and you would be queen."

"Would I be like your cousin? Like Vera? Going to luncheons and sitting on charity boards?"

"My mother did." His voice cooled even as anger leapt into his eyes. "She served Rodina. Her work was no less important."

"And from what I remember your father saying, she loved it. She was good at it because she loved it. But for me…" Her voice trailed off as she sought to put her chaotic thoughts into words, to explain what she was feeling. "What about economic forums? The trade summit we attended? Would I just be an ornament or actually serve the people?"

His frown deepened. "My mother was no mere ornament. The queen is a figurehead. A leader who serves the people, too."

She stood frozen in place. Part of her, the part that had never stopped loving him, urged her to accept the ring. To be with the man she had fallen for. But the woman she'd become, the woman she was growing into, hesitated. She had just broken free of the expectations of others. She knew people like Julius's mother, like Vera, were needed.

Did it make her selfish, then, that she wanted something different?

Excluding the details of the role, was accepting his ring, especially one tied to duty with no room for love, just going back to an old pattern? Saying yes with the hope that someone might one day love her in return, even as she lived out her days as an ornament instead of an equal partner?

His lips thinned. "I take it marrying me is not what you want then."

She threw her hands up in the air. "I don't know, Julius! I've always tried to live for others' expectations. To be dismissed one week and then proposed to the next, because I'm valuable…" She nearly choked on the last word. "I know public appearances are important. Charities are critical. But to have that be my life…my only life…"

"It's more than that." Thunder moved across his face, darkened his eyes as a vein pulsed in his throat. "I thought you would understand duty."

"I do. But… I want more than just duty, Julius. You know the kind of woman I am, how much I read and re-search and stay involved with what's going on with our country. Whether or not I'm queen, the woman who is by your side deserves to have a choice in how she serves."

"Being a royal rarely provides choices."

"But there is more than one way to rule," she insisted. "You taught me that, showed me that every time you and father disagreed on something. Why can't a queen do more than be a public figurehead?"

"I'm not saying she couldn't."

"Except you have it all planned out." Her heartbeat in her throat so hard it nearly made her choke. "Planned it without talking to me, without thinking about who I am, what I might want, what I could give back."

He stared at her, his amber eyes glittering. "I have let down my guard with you more than I have anyone else."

"I know."

She reached up to lay her hand on his jaw. He pulled back, a fraction of an inch, but it could have been a mile for how much distance it put between them. Hurt, she snatched her hand back and crossed her arms over her chest, the thin silk of her robe cold against her breasts.

"When I get married, I want it to be because I love someone and he loves me. I want it to be a partnership. Not a loveless transaction where I have little to no say. Where the rest of my life is already laid out for me."

The snap of the ring box closing echoed in the room.

"If there is even the barest hint of that being a possibility, then your answer was the right one."

Ice dripped from every word. The brutal prince was back in full force, his eyes hard as flint, his face carved from granite.

For one moment, she contemplated telling him what she needed. What she wanted. What could be if she could have just a little time to think, to process.

And then fear raised its ugly head once more, fear and years of pain, of disappointment.

She ignored him and walked back toward the bed. She plucked her sundress off the ground, the sunshine yellow a brutal contrast to how dark she felt inside. She slid out of the robe and pulled her dress on. When she turned back, Julius was watching her, his face cold, one hand wrapped around the ring box.

Silence reigned between them. Both of them so angry. So hurt. Neither willing to yield.

She left the room without saying a word. She didn't know what else there was left to say. In less than five minutes her one suitcase was packed, the dress stuffed inside in favor of a T-shirt and shorts, her hair pulled back into a bun. She moved to the window and gazed out over the terrace, the beach, the view of the ocean, for the last time.

Her phone felt heavy in her hand as she dialed.

"Esme." Burak's voice boomed over the line. "How are—?"

"His Highness is in Grenada. Dove Villa off Prickly Bay."

Silence followed.

"Burak?"

"What—"

"His Highness was attacked in London. He tracked me down to Grenada and hired me to be his temporary bodyguard while he healed."

Burak's expletive echoed from thousands of miles away, followed by a series of rapid-fire questions.

"You'll have to ask him."

She hung up, swallowed the guilt that she had just betrayed him and walked out with suitcase in hand. He stood in his doorway, dressed in nothing but lounge pants that hung low on his hips.

"I do owe you thanks," she said quietly as she neared him.

"You owe me nothing."

"But I do. If you hadn't reassigned me, I don't how long I would have drifted along in a state of complacency." She smiled sadly. "It was the shock I needed to realize something needed to change in my life."

He looked down at her suitcase.

"You're running away again."

She bristled.

And you're not stopping me. Again.

Then she stifled her anger. Anger had gotten her into this mess in the first place. Had she kept her cool when he'd arrived on Grenada, she would have made the call far sooner.

"I'm making a choice."

He stared at her, chest rising and falling, but he kept his hands clenched by his sides. The ring box had disappeared.

"I'm…" A ringing cut him off. He pulled his phone out of his pocket and glanced at the screen. His face hardened as his head snapped up.

"You called the palace."

She raised her chin. "It's what I should have done in the first place."

Was it pain that flashed in his eyes? Or had she mistaken anger for hurt? Regardless, she had done her duty, and severed any connections remaining between them.

It was like walking through a fog, she thought, as she moved toward the end of the hall, one that made the world around her seem blurred. Elements of familiar pain wove through the ache pulsing in her bones.

She paused where the hallway, turned and looked back.

"You'll make a wonderful king."

Framed in the doorway to his room, with the ocean rising and falling beyond the window, his dark blond hair brushed back from his forehead and shoulders thrown back despite the weight that rested on them, he looked every inch the heir apparent.

She executed a formal bow.

"Your Highness."

And then she was gone.

CHAPTER SEVENTEEN

JULIUS TUGGED ON the rope attached to the mainsail—*mainsheet, not rope*, he silently corrected himself—and savored the thrill as the sail pressed out. The boat picked up speed, curving around the northern tip of Rodina. The palace stood tall and proud nearly two hundred feet above his head, perched on a cliff that overlooked the Atlantic Ocean to the north and the west, and the distant, hazy coastline of Portugal to the east.

It had been nearly three weeks since he'd been back. Three weeks since Esmerelda had left. His fury, the gut-wrenching sensation of betrayal that she had called the palace had been short-lived.

There had been nothing left for him on Grenada. Nothing but memories of a fleeting time that he suspected was the happiest he had been in a long time.

Perhaps the happiest he would ever be.

He'd returned Burak's call after Esmerelda had walked out, assuming the mantle of leader as if it had never slipped away. Within an hour he'd been on a private jet flying across the Caribbean Sea, despite his head of security's insolent insistence that he wait for a team to come get him and ensure he was fit to fly after his attack.

His new head of security had greeted him at the airport. A tall bear of a man, Burak was intelligent, shrewd and relentless. He'd asked numerous questions, ranging from the hotel Julius had stayed at in London to the doctor he'd seen on Grenada. Questions Julius had answered concisely as he'd reviewed schedules, proposed legislation and news stories, catching up on the pieces of his life he'd missed out on the past week.

The only thing he deflected on was his and Esmerelda's relationship. When Burak had prodded, Julius had speared him with an icy gaze and said, "If you want to keep your job, you will never, ever suggest that Miss Clark behaved in a manner unbecoming her position."

Judging by his narrowed eyes and tight mouth, Burak hadn't liked his answer. But he'd accepted it with a grudging nod before moving on to other questions.

The only other person who had been told the full truth of what had transpired was his father. When the plane had landed, Julius had requested an immediate audience with his father. Francisco had greeted him at the palace, his hug sparking both affection and guilt. Once they'd been secure in the privacy of Francisco's study, he'd asked after Esmerelda and if she had accepted his ring.

Julius had hesitated. Francisco had leaned forward, lacing his fingers together as if to stop himself from reaching out to his only child.

"What's on your mind, son?"

He told his father everything, from waking up in his hotel room to Esmerelda's departure and everything in between. Francisco had listened. It wasn't until Julius reached the end that he had finally spoken.

"That's rough."

The simple summation had made Julius laugh and broken the tension. His father hadn't pushed, hadn't berated or lectured him. He'd simply asked if there was anything he could do and, when Julius had responded in the negative, said he was always available if Julius needed to talk.

Before Julius had left, his father had circled the desk and enveloped him in a tight hug that spoke louder than any words could say. The sheen in Francisco's eyes, the slight fear of what might have happened in that London alleyway, went unsaid but not unrecognized.

The quiet support, the subtle demonstrations of love, struck him anew. After his mother's death, he had shunned all emotional connection. His eyes had always been fixed on the future, never the present or the past. Tasks, lists, always having a goal to work toward, had kept him focused. Kept his heart safe, even from his own father, who had done nothing but offer him quiet yet steady love and support.

Until her.

Every time he thought of how she had bowed to him, hurt once more by his cruel words yet still so proud before she had walked out of his life once again, his chest tightened until he could barely breathe. Nights were the hardest, especially reaching as he woke and having his fingers brush cool, empty sheets instead of Esme's warmth.

He maintained a façade throughout his days as he eased into his duties, professional yet with a touch of the humanness he'd discovered in his weeks on the island. More smiles, the occasional joke. It was amusing, and gratifying, to see people exchange wide-eyed glances as they wondered what had happened to finally make Prince Julius's cold exterior thaw.

The beach appeared, the black sand a sharp contrast to Grenada's powdery white shores. He angled the boat toward the dock and winced as the hull hit harder than he'd intended. But, he reminded himself as he tied off the boat and stepped onto the dock, he had made vast improvements. It had shocked a number of people when Prince Julius, renowned for doing nothing but working, eating and sleeping, had booked private sailing lessons.

He'd wanted to do something, anything outside of his role as prince. Being on the water, feeling the familiar rise and fall of the waves, smelling the salt air, had been a comfort he hadn't even realized he'd needed until he'd first boarded with his instructor. He'd dedicated an hour every night to practicing.

When he'd taken the boat out for his first solo trip around the north end of Rodina two days ago, he'd nearly called her. Had wanted to share it with her.

But he hadn't. She had left. He had offered more of himself to her than he had to anyone since his mother had passed. Had finally risked it all and made a decision based on his heart.

It hadn't been enough.

You know that's not all of it.

He closed his eyes and breathed in the scent of the ocean. The heat of the sun seeped into his skin, bringing memories of a tiny island in the Atlantic up from the depths. He opened his eyes and started up the stone steps carved into the cliff. He reached the towering gate at the top of the stairs and punched in the security code. Heat from the sun warmed his back. The gate creaked as he pushed it open, clanged as he shut it. He focused on the sound of his feet on the pavestones, the gentle swishing as an afternoon breeze stirred the flower-tipped stalks of lavender that lined the walkway.

The past invaded. He couldn't stop the image of her stricken expression when he'd told her his reasons for why she would make the perfect queen. As the feeling of being rejected had faded, reality had sunk in, cold and vicious. He had done what so many had done to her in the past, especially her parents; he had reduced her from a dynamic, interesting woman to a list of qualifications. Had taken her comments about being an ornament as a personal slight against his mother and all the good she had done instead of hearing Esmerelda's words.

In the moment, when Esmerelda had looked at him and asked for more, he'd felt the pain of rejection like a knife to the heart. The pieces of himself he had shared hadn't been enough for her. The risk he'd taken deemed inadequate.

But then he remembered her face. Her own sense of rejection. His inability to voice the true depths of his feelings for her.

It had been reasonable for him to withdraw after his mother had been yanked from him so quickly, here one moment alive and happy, then gone in a matter of weeks. Yet, he grudgingly admitted as he walked into the palace gardens, it had also become an excuse over the years. It was easier to stay aloof, to never feel the gut-wrenching grief that had nearly consumed him when his mother had passed.

Until now. Until a different kind of grief shadowed his every step, haunted his waking hours, plagued his dreams. The grief of having held someone he deeply cared about and letting her slip away not once, but twice.

"You look terrible."

Julius looked up as his father walked into the garden.

"Recovering from a traumatic head injury is a good excuse for not looking my best."

"Hmm." Francisco glanced down at a stalk of lavender. "I rarely come here. It's a nice spot, though."

"It is."

Francisco moved to a spot in the wall with a wrought-iron fence instead of the exquisitely painted tiles that covered the garden walls. Beyond the fence the ground rushed out in an explosion of green before sloping sharply down toward another beach. The waves rose and fell in gentle swells, the water rising up onto the dark sand before receding back into the ocean.

Julius joined his father at the fence and stared out. Hard to believe that a week ago he had been on the other side of this ocean struggling with the idea of his identity revolving around a title.

"I can feel you thinking too hard."

Francisco scoffed. "No such thing. But," he added with a slight smile, "if I were thinking, it might be to ask what thoughts you have toward moving forward."

A stone settled in the pit of Julius's stomach.

"Let me know if you have any suitable candidates in mind."

"Are you sure?"

"Yes."

The word rolled off Julius's tongue, but with a distinct lack of conviction. Once he had believed the sentiment of finding the best wife to suit Rodina's advancement with his entire being. It had been easier to see a future marriage and even a family as for the better of the country rather than an investment he would make on his own.

But now, the thought of kissing another woman, sliding the ring onto her finger, sharing children with her, made him feel empty, like someone had hollowed out his chest and left nothing behind except sorrow.

"What of Esmerelda?"

Julius's head snapped up.

"I don't want to talk about her."

Francisco ignored his son's icy tone.

"Do you realize that you coming to ask my permission to propose to Esmerelda is the first thing you've asked of me since your mother passed? It's always been the job, what's best for the country, best for the people. Another reason why you'll be a good king. But," Francisco added as Julius started to interrupt, "how good can a king be if he works himself to the bone and becomes too tired, too worn down, to be a good leader?"

Julius grimaced.

"You sound like her."

"I've spent a lot of time thinking this past year. A lot," Francisco repeated as he once again looked out over the sea. "I've also watched you. I noticed long ago how you were around Miss Clark. It was as if your edges had been smoothed out."

Slowly, Julius reached into his pocket. His fingers wrapped around the jeweler's box. How many times had he pulled it out over the past few days, holding it up to the light, running his fingers over the diamond, the aquamarine gems, the tiny pearls. Miss Smythe had answered his numerous questions during their initial consultation, helped him pick the gems and stones: aquamarine for the happiness she'd brought to his life. Pearl for the wisdom she had shared with him as they'd talked of Rodina.

And the diamond, speckled. Flawed, like Esmerelda saw herself. Yet to him, beautiful beyond measure.

The longer you look, the more you see.

"She is an incredible woman." Francisco tilted his head to one side. "Did you tell her you loved her?"

The edges of the ring box cut into his palms as he gripped it tighter. Did he love her? He cared about her, yes. But as he turned his father's question over in his mind, certainty flooded his veins. His feelings for Esmerelda went far deeper than affection. He desired her, craved her presence, missed her saucy smile and joyful laugh. Yet he trusted her, too, not just with his life but his heart. That she cared just as deeply about Rodina as he did was another bond that he had at first categorized as making her an ideal queen, not recognizing that it bound them together, too.

"I told her I cared about her."

Francisco threw back his head and laughed. Julius frowned at him.

"Helpful, Pai. Very helpful."

Francisco's laughter quieted as a nostalgic smile tugged at his lips.

"I wish I had had more time with your mother. So many things I wish we had done. We weren't in love when we got engaged," he said. "I did it for duty. But when we did fall in love..." His voice trailed off as his gaze turned distant.

Julius smiled slightly. "She told me."

"One thing I never regretted, though, once I realized how I felt, was telling her every day how I felt about her."

Francisco left, leaving Julius alone once more in the garden.

He pulled the box out of his pocket and opened it. The ring glinted in the sunlight. The longer he stared at it, the more a fool he felt. Yes, Esmerelda had the potential to be a queen Rodina deserved. But she was also the only woman he wanted. The only woman he had ever loved. She deserved to hear that, to hear that he wanted her by his side because of who she was, not because of what she had to offer. That he wouldn't just shove her into a box of his own making but give her the power to lead her own life.

She deserved the choice to accept him, or reject him,

but with a full picture of what he was offering. He didn't like the latter possibility, despised the nervousness at giving up his power and surrendering to his emotions.

But, he thought with renewed determination as he tucked the ring back into his pocket, if anyone was worth the risk of opening up his heart to, it was Esmerelda.

His phone dinged. He pulled it out of his pocket, read the email that had just landed in his inbox.

And smiled.

CHAPTER EIGHTEEN

"Miss Clark?"

Esme stood and smiled at the young man who gave her a friendly smile as he walked out of a boardroom.

"Yes," she replied as she shook his hand.

"Welcome to Executive Security."

She stepped inside and blinked at the jaw-dropping view of New York City's Brooklyn Bridge and the East River flowing beneath it.

Two other people, a man and a woman, sat at the table. They both gave her pleasant smiles as she sat in the offered chair.

"We've spoken to your former employer."

Her smile froze on her face.

"Yes?"

"Exemplary," the woman said. "They were sorry to lose you."

Relief made her so weak she had to resist the urge to sink back into the plush office chair.

"It was hard to leave."

"Why did you?" the man who'd greeted her asked.

"I've lived in Rodina my whole life. I needed a change of scenery. And my mother lives here."

Not that it had impacted her decision in the slightest. She'd reached out to let her mother know she was in town, her first time in the States in nearly ten years. Her mother, predictably, had been on a cruise in the Bahamas and rushed to get off the phone and back to her husband.

Instead of making her feel sorry for herself, it had been cathartic in a way. Her mother would always be the way she was. Her focus on herself, her inability to enjoy motherhood, hadn't been Esme's fault. Neither was her father's inability to see her as anything more than her accomplishments.

Something Julius's blunt assessment had helped her realize.

She swallowed hard. Julius cropped up far too often in her thoughts. She shoved him away and tried to focus on the people in front of her. But doubt kept plaguing her.

Did she even want another bodyguard position? Would that make her happy? She'd originally gone into the profession to make her father happy, but now...

They asked her a few questions, but she could tell it was mostly to tick the boxes. Whoever they'd spoken to in Rodina, coupled with the fact that she had been on a security detail for an actual prince, had impressed them. She'd built up the kind of reputation that made her the perfect candidate for any security job.

"Last question," the woman asked. "Where do you see yourself in five years?"

Esme froze.

"I'm..." She offered up a slight smile, one that hopefully would pacify. "I'm not sure. Leaving Rodina was a big step for me."

"Of course." The woman returned her smile with a kind one of her own. "How about what you want out of your life? What do you want out of your career? What's important to you?"

Julius.

The sudden surety of her unspoken answer floored her. She wanted Julius. Loved him. Had had the chance to be with him and had shunned it out of fear of losing her newfound independence, of being shoved into yet another box and smothered with someone else's expectations.

When he'd proposed, she had been so focused on how he'd had everything planned out, a plan he hadn't bothered to ask her about, that she had let pain overtake her, keep her from telling him her own feelings and what she needed. What would allow her to accept his proposal.

And Rodina…being a queen, leading a country, might not be her first choice of a job. It would come with scrutiny, long hours and rules. So many rules. But she had been so afraid of accepting the role in the form Julius had presented it to her that she hadn't stopped to think about what she could do. What she would do if given the chance to be a leader.

She hadn't stopped to talk to Julius, to ask him, to challenge him. She'd been so afraid of what his answer might have been that she had chosen to run instead of standing and fighting for herself, for them and what they could be.

"Miss Clark?"

Esme blinked. Three faces were regarding her with mixtures of concern and confusion.

"I'm sorry." She stood and smoothed her hands over the bottom of her suit jacket. "I don't think this role is for me. I thought I needed something else in my life. But it turns out I was wrong. Thank you for your time. I'm sorry to have wasted it."

And with that she turned and walked out.

Her foot tapped an impatient rhythm as the elevator descended. She needed to do something, find a way to meet with Julius and tell him everything. Would he accept a phone call? A text message?

No. That was the coward's way out. This was the kind of conversation that required them to be face-to-face. She pulled out her phone. Her fingers flew over the screen as she typed out an email request for a meeting at His Highness's earliest convenience.

Then, before she could lose her nerve, she hit "send."

Forty-eight hours later, Esme stared at the key in her hand as she stood in front of the hotel elevator. The number embedded in the platinum card stared back at her, taunted her.

Room 333. The penthouse suite where she and Julius had spent the night together.

Did Fate just have it out for her?

No, she thought as she rubbed at her temple. It was only natural that the suite be rented out to royalty, politicians and other important guests. With its location at the top of The Martinique, it was not only well protected but offered exquisite views of Paris and the Eiffel Tower.

A sigh escaped her. When she had received the email requesting her presence in Paris to meet with the king less than an hour after she'd emailed Julius, her stomach had dropped to somewhere in the vicinity of her feet. Did the king want to question her? Grill her as to why she had spent a week in Grenada with his son? Or perhaps he had found out about her affair with Julius. She no longer worked for the royal security team, so no risk of getting fired. But he could still make life very difficult for her.

Worse was the possibility that Julius had forwarded her

email to his father and asked him to intervene. Her email had been formal, simply asking for a meeting. She should have gone through the proper channels, but she hadn't been able to bring herself to email the public relations office or his secretary. Burak hadn't called or texted since she'd called him to let him know where Julius was. Her father had also been strangely silent, his incessant phone calls dropping off.

The possibility that someone had uncovered her week with Julius had dogged her steps the past two days, from the soaring steel towers of New York City to the sprawling *arrondissements* of Paris.

She stepped inside and held up the key card. The elevator rose, carrying her closer and closer to the mysterious meeting with King Francisco. She had met the king on a few occasions. He had even come to her hospital room to thank her when she had been recovering from the parade accident. A skilled but kind, compassionate leader.

Would he show her kindness now? Or savagery as he protected his son and the reputation of the crown?

The elevator dinged. The doors slid open again. She tamped down her nervousness and stepped inside.

The suite was exactly the same. Warm wood floors gleaming under the golden rays of the setting sun. Ivory-colored furniture offset by red and blue pillows that added color to the elegant surroundings. A fireplace trimmed in white, the hearth filled with a vase of flowers for the summer season instead of burning logs.

And beyond the sitting room, glass doors thrown open to the balcony and the Eiffel Tower standing proudly over Paris.

She'd stood in that doorway, just out of sight, with Julius at her back. He'd slid her shirt up and over her head, placing heated, sensual kisses on her neck as he'd undone the clasp on her bra and then reached out around to fill his hands—

"Your Highness?" she called out, partially to stop the flow of memories and partially because she realized, with a quick glance, that the suite was empty.

No one answered.

Frowning, she pulled up the email on her phone and reread it. Labeled with the royal family's official seal at the top, the email was brief. It requested her presence on the twelfth of June at seven o'clock in the penthouse suite of The Martinique in Paris for a meeting with His Majesty the King.

"I prefer this meeting to Grenada."

Esme's head snapped up. She stared as Julius walked out of the door that led to the bedroom. His dress shirt showcased the breadth of his shoulders. He'd rolled the sleeves up to his elbows, the white material stark against his tan skin. Her eyes traveled up, over his chest and up his neck to his heartbreakingly familiar brown eyes.

"You...where is..."

"I think I need to mark this on the calendar, too. The first time Esmerelda Clark stuttered."

She heard the teasing in his voice and resisted. She squared her shoulders and drew herself up, shoving away all of her emotions.

"Your Highness. My apologies for intruding. I received an email—"

"May I see it?"

She stifled her irritation at being interrupted and handed over her phone, taking care to ensure her fingers didn't brush his. His eyes moved over the words.

"Ah, yes. I think there's a typo."

"A typo?"

"Yes, it shouldn't have said 'His Majesty the King.' It should have read 'His Royal Highness the Crown Prince.'" He looked up, a wicked gleam in his eyes. "Oops."

Confused, unsure of what to expect, overwhelmed by the memories surrounding her, she took a step back. Julius's arm shot out, his hand grabbing her elbow. Words of protest died on her lips as he yanked her against him before sliding one arm across her back and another beneath her knees. With a small shriek, she found herself lifted into the arms of Crown Prince Julius Carvalho.

"Put me down."

"Not until you promise not to run away."

She groaned and closed her eyes, trying desperately to ignore how good it felt to be cradled by him once more.

"I don't understand."

She felt him lean in closer, felt the heat of his body. A moment later his forehead touched hers and she drew in a shuddering breath. That such a simple touch could affect her so much frightened her.

"Esmerelda. Look at me."

She slowly opened her eyes but kept her gaze fixed over his shoulder on the Eiffel Tower.

"I can't look at you, Julius. Not yet. I know I requested a meeting, but I thought I would have time to prepare myself."

"Fine. Then just listen."

Perhaps it was worse not to look at him. Because not looking at him aroused her other senses, made her more aware of the rumble of his voice in his chest, the cords of muscle in his arms as he gripped her close.

He walked with her to the glass doors. She started to protest as he walked onto the balcony, then stopped as he sat down on a lounge, still cradling her like she was a precious jewel.

"You were right."

"Of course I was."

She felt his smile.

"I hurt you."

She started, but kept her gaze averted. Her heart thudded in her chest. This had been part of the risk she had accepted when she'd sent that email. Telling him what she needed, sharing her own feelings, could still result in heartbreak. But at least she would have given it her all, tried to advocate for herself instead of simply submitting or running away.

"Yes. You did." She let out a breath. "Although I imagine I did my fair share of hurting."

"Yes." He pressed his cheek against her hair, a shuddering sigh whispering over her face. "I took away your choice. Again."

Her eyes grew hot.

"Yes. But I—"

"Let me apologize, Esmerelda. Then you can have your turn to grovel."

She faced him then, lightly punched his shoulder. "Who said I'm going to grovel?"

"Call it intuition." His smile disappeared as his eyes darkened with regret. "I wanted you so badly, Esmerelda. I knew I could make it work, so I did. I thought you wanted me, too."

"I—"

He kissed her then, a smoldering kiss she felt all the way to her toes.

"Whether you did or not, I assumed. I made plans for you. I've been leading for so long I did what I always do.

Make plans, execute them. When you didn't jump at the chance to wear the ring, I took it as you rejecting what I had offered. A monumental offer, given my predilection of avoiding emotion. But," he said as he kissed the tip of her nose, "I was still holding back. I told myself I was risking enough. Giving enough."

She swallowed hard. "It wasn't fair of me to push for so much so soon. That doesn't mean," she said quickly as he opened his mouth to interject, "I don't deserve it. But you did offer me a great deal, Julius, and I let my own past get the better of me instead of giving it some time or having a conversation. I tried to be independent instead of listening to my own heart. I asked questions, but I didn't tell you what I needed from you, what I could bring to throne." She lowered her head. "You were right. I did run away."

"Perhaps if I had told you…"

His voice trailed off. His arms tightened around her as he stood and carried her to the railing. The Eiffel Tower came to life as he set her on her feet, light glittering across the iron structure.

"I love you." He lowered his forehead to hers. "I've loved you for so long."

Happiness spread through her, swirling through her chest and filling her body until she felt as if she could float. He cradled her face with such tenderness she couldn't hold back a tear from escaping.

He swiped away the tear with a finger. "I suspect I've made you cry far too many tears in our time together."

"Yes." She reached up and let her hand settle on his cheek. "But love often involves tears. And I do love you, Julius."

A harsh breath escaped him.

"Just like I didn't know what I had done to deserve

such loyalty from a young woman, I don't know how I deserve your love."

"It was nothing you had to earn, Julius. I gave it freely because of who you are." She swallowed past the thickness in her throat. "I should have told you in Grenada. Should have told you what I needed from you, what I wanted. But I was too afraid. I accused you of not talking to me, and then I did the exact same thing. You offered me so much then, and I was so wrapped up in my own pain I could only see my own fears and not what you had overcome to even make that proposal." She bit down on her lower lip, looked away. "I'm sorry."

He grasped her chin in his fingers and tilted her face up so he could look her in the eye.

"I told you that day in the hospital that I was humbled to be the recipient of such loyalty. Today," he whispered softly as he leaned in, "I am humbled to be loved by such an incredible woman. One who gives despite having so much withheld. One who can look at herself and what she needs to change, who wants to grow beyond her boundaries or the restrictions others place on her. One who I love deeply and who I can only hope will one day forgive me for holding myself back."

The words drifted around her, beautiful words that made hope and longing surge in her chest so fiercely in that moment she felt like she could fly.

Except reality held her back. He might love her now. But what did that mean? A tragic parting like the princess and the newspaper reporter in the old black-and-white movie she had watched on repeat in the late hours of the night, where they had admitted their love for one another and shared a bittersweet kiss before the princess had returned to her royal life?

"Julius, I... I appreciate you sharing how you feel."

One eyebrow shot up.

"'Appreciate' is not exactly the kind of sentiment a man wants to hear after he's just professed love to a woman."

"How about 'I love you, Julius'?"

He nodded once, then suddenly released her.

"One moment."

He disappeared. Flustered, she stepped away and moved to the balcony. She smoothed the skirt of her dress, focused on the lights of the Tower. Contentment settled over her, along with a peace that steadied her racing heart and brought a smile to her lips. For once, she was exactly where she wanted to be. He loved her. She loved him. She wanted to be with him. Whatever came next would come in its own time.

Footsteps sounded behind her. One deep breath, then another. She turned, ready to face him.

Her heart nearly burst as her mind registered that Julius was no longer standing but kneeling before her. In his hand lay the black jewelry box, the lid open and the speckled diamond gleaming with the rosy lights of a Parisian sunset.

"I'm not just asking you to become my wife, Esmerelda. What I'm asking is so much more, and it may be too much." Love burned in his eyes as he took her hand in his. "Just as you were ready to move forward, to be your own person, I'm asking you to become a servant of the people of Rodina. A servant to the country and all that entails. It has its merits, yes, but it also has hardships. Being under constant scrutiny, having your every choice questioned."

"You're not exactly selling this proposal," she said with a soft laugh. "And I'm nervous, Julius. I don't know how to be a queen."

"I am, too. But you are not only the woman I want.

You're the queen Rodina deserves." His grip tightened on hers. "You love Rodina. You're intelligent. You care. Those traits mean more than anything anyone else could have brought to an arranged marriage. I believe that whole-heartedly. Which means I need to let go, to let you carve out your own path when it comes to your role if you choose to accept it."

Her eyes widened at the magnitude of what he was saying. That he would give up control, trust her to make her own choices as she helped him lead the country he loved, meant more than any ring ever could have.

The last weight hanging from her heart loosened, then fell away.

"Julius…"

"Maybe that's not enough," he continued. "But I can't live with knowing I had the chance to ask you to be my wife, to be the woman I want by my side, and didn't. I would rather move on knowing I took the risk, told you how much I love you, and you said no than go the rest of my life wondering what could have been."

The seeds of hope that had been steadily growing burst inside her chest. Her smile grew until it nearly hurt, she was smiling so hard.

"Tell me that's a yes, Esmerelda."

She nodded, barely able to choke out a "yes." He slid the ring onto her finger then stood, sweeping her into his arms and pulling her flush against him as he leaned down and sealed their engagement with a sensual, possessive kiss. She flung her arms around his neck and kissed him back, laughing against his lips as he picked her up and spun her around in a circle.

"It fits," she said, holding up her hand as he set her back on her feet. The diamond glittered, the tiny little black flecks dancing mischievously within the crystalline depths. The pearls gleamed, an innocent touch of beauty, while the aquamarine stones sparkled in the sun.

"It was always for you." He caught her chin in his hand, brought his lips to hers once more and kissed her until she clung to him. "I went to London to purchase a ring. I had a detective track you to Grenada, intended to follow you apologize and propose to you. Show you, not just tell you." He grasped her hand in his and raised it to his mouth. "This ring was designed for you, Esmerelda. Pearls for the wisdom and grace you carry, aquamarine for hope and happiness, and a salt-and-pepper diamond. Imperfectly beautiful, with flaws that make it stronger. And," he added with a kiss to her nose, "because it reminded me of your freckles. Your beautiful freckles."

She did cry then, tears coursing down her cheeks as he held her. What greater gift could she have asked for than a man who loved her, truly loved her and all her imperfections?

"I love you, Julius."

"And I love you, Esmerelda." He grasped her shoulders, held her back. "You're sure?"

"Yes. I know it won't be easy. It will take some getting used to. But I'm sure."

He watched her, eyes darting over her face as if looking for a sign that this was too good to be true.

"And this is what you want?"

"Yes." She stepped closer then, bringing her hands up to frame his face. "I emailed you from New York. I interviewed for a job there and they asked me what I wanted from my life. All I could think of was you. I almost told you back in Grenada that I wanted to be with you, but I was terrified that if I told you I wanted your love, it would be too much.

"Marrying you, becoming a queen, doesn't mean I still can't be myself. I get to combine one of my greatest passions with a new career. And," she added as she raised up on her toes, "I get to marry the man I love."

He crushed her to him.

"My queen," he murmured into her hair, "and tomorrow the whole world will know it."

"Tomorrow?"

"An engagement announcement, if you're willing. I want the world to know you're mine."

His possessive tone thrilled her, sent little sparks dancing through her veins.

"I'm more than willing."

"Good." He leaned, pressed his lips to her forehead. "Tonight, however," he murmured as he kissed her cheek, the tip of her nose, "I want you all to myself."

She took his hand, led him back into the bedroom as the lights of the Tower sparkled behind them. She laid on the bed, her breath catching in her chest as he lay next to her and pulled her body against his. As he lowered his mouth to hers, she smiled.

"There's nowhere else I'd rather be."

EPILOGUE

One year later

ESME STARED AT her reflection in the tri-mirror.

"Joana," she breathed as she smoothed her hands over the silk skirt, "this is beautiful."

The bodice of her wedding dress, fashioned from the most exquisite lace, featured a sweetheart neckline with a touch of sexiness. The fitted waist flared into a stunning skirt that swept down to the floor and pooled behind her. Swaths of lace flowed from her shoulders down her back like fairy wings.

"You make it beautiful, Your Highness."

Esme glanced over her shoulder at Joana and her sister, Hanna. The two had been flown in a week earlier to partake in the festivities leading up to the royal wedding, as well as to serve as two of Esme's bridesmaids. The three had grown close over the past year, with Joana officially named as the preferred designer of Princess Esmerelda.

Even though she wouldn't officially receive her title until after the wedding ceremony was complete, the press had jumped on her future moniker and run with it. The engagement announcement for a prince and his bodyguard had entranced the public. A news outlet had rediscovered the video of Esme pushing Julius out of harm's way during the parade. Rodina had been catapulted into the international spotlight as the media swooned over the "storybook romance." Leaked details from London about Julius's brush with a mugger, who had eventually been caught using his credit card, had added intrigue to their love story.

A love that had taken them back to Grenada less than two months after they'd left, where they'd joined Aroldo and his family for Spicemas. Amongst the parades, dancing and celebrations, their friendship with Aroldo, Hanna and Joana had been solidified.

A whistle cut through the room.

"You look incredible," Burak said as he walked into the room. He winked at her. "Your Highness."

"Not quite yet," she replied with a laugh directed at her "man of honor." Burak had taken one look at her and Julius together and promptly forgiven her duplicity. He'd been amused by her request that he be in her wedding party, although it was a duty he had also taken seriously.

The delicate melody of a violin trickled in. Esme's breath caught.

"Is it time?"

Joana nodded, her eyes bright.

"Are you ready?"

She'd been ready ever since Julius had slipped the ring on her finger.

She accepted her bouquet of lilies from Hanna and moved to the door. A moment later her father appeared, his silver hair combed back from his forehead. His eyes widened.

"Esmerelda…"

Her breath caught at the naked emotion in his eyes. When she'd returned to Rodina, her father had at first been coldly angry with her for deserting. Even learning that she was engaged to a prince hadn't softened him.

But then one day she'd caught him staring at her during a formal dinner. The next day he'd called on her in the royal apartment that had been set aside for her as the fiancée of the crown prince.

"You looked happy," he'd said, his voice rough. "I don't think I ever saw you happy before."

"I wasn't."

He'd nodded. "I'm sorry."

It had been a new beginning for them, one that had evolved and strengthened over the past year. Her relationship with her mother was still distant. Aside from her mother's initial excitement over shopping for a wedding dress, eclipsed fairly quickly by Esme's insistence on using Joana as her designer, her mother had played her usual role and stayed in New York, only flying in last night to attend the ceremony.

A part of Esme would always long for something more. But then she would look around at the people she had in her life: Julius. His father, a man she still struggled to call "Francisco" or "Father" instead of His Majesty. Aroldo, Hanna and Joana. Her own father. Burak. Even the mysterious and talented Miss Smythe was in attendance for the wedding.

And she had purpose. Julius had encouraged her to carve out her own role in the palace, one that would both support Rodina but also bring her happiness. She'd accompanied Julius to an international energy summit and debated legislation on healthcare with members of Parliament. But she'd also stepped back from her fear of being shoved into a box and tried some of the community activities Julius's cousin Vera engaged in. She'd come to enjoy serving on the board for the library, and collaborated with several local authors and a publisher to host an international literary festival the following year. Whether it would succeed in drawing in guests from Europe and beyond like she hoped remained to be seen.

But she was trying. She was doing something with her life. She was truly, deeply blessed.

The music swelled. Her father held out his arm.

"Are you ready?"

"Yes."

They moved into the hall and stopped outside the massive wooden doors leading into the palace chapel. A moment later the doors were flung open, revealing an aisle strewn with red rose petals. Burak escorted Joana and Hanna down the aisle.

And then she saw him. Julius stood at the altar, incredibly handsome in a black tuxedo. When their eyes met, he smiled. She smiled back, her heart nearly bursting with love. A collective sigh moved through the room, although she barely heard it.

They moved down the aisle. At last, she stood in front of Julius. He shook her father's hand as she passed off her bouquet, then led her up the stairs to the altar.

"You're beautiful, Esmerelda." He raised her hand to his lips, kissed her knuckles.

"It's not quite the time to kiss the bride," the priest said with an indulgent smile, much to the amusement of the guests.

Esme barely heard the words spoken as he grasped her hands, his eyes bright with love. When he said "I do" in a clear, ringing voice, she couldn't stop the tears that spilled down her cheeks.

"I now pronounce you man and wife. Now you may kiss the bride."

Julius pulled her close, resting his forehead against hers for one blissful second, and then pressed his lips to hers.

"You were wrong," he whispered against her mouth.

"How so?"

"I'd say this is as close to a fairy tale as it gets."

* * * * *

If this Emmy Grayson story left you longing for more, then be sure to check out the first instalment of the Diamonds of the Rich and Famous *trilogy* Accidentally Wearing the Argentinian's Ring

And don't miss her previous books for Harlequin Presents!

A Cinderella for the Prince's Revenge
The Prince's Pregnant Secretary
Cinderella Hired for His Revenge
His Assistant's New York Awakening
An Heir Made in Hawaii

Available now!

HARLEQUIN
Reader Service

Enjoyed your book?

Try the perfect subscription for Romance readers and get
more great books like this delivered right to your door.

See why over 10+ million readers have tried
Harlequin Reader Service.

Start with a Free Welcome Collection with free books and a gift—valued over $20.

Choose any series in print or ebook.
See website for details and order today:

TryReaderService.com/subscriptions

RSBPA24R